Sara had to admit it tickled her to pieces that Cody remembered her likes and dislikes

Him—she liked very much.

Amusement gleamed in Cody's eyes. "You want to eat at another restaurant, don't you? How about filet mignon and a lobster tail with drawn butter? Tiramisu for dessert sound good?"

She leaned toward him. "You do understand this is totally about sex," she whispered and was rewarded with a look of shock. "You don't have to wine and dine me."

He opened his mouth, but nothing came out.

Sara laughed, not feeling quite as brazen as she sounded. "Come on. Admit it. That's really why you got on that plane and came here to Atlanta. It doesn't have anything to do with that ol' legal case. It was to see me, right?"

"You're crazy."

"You're crazy about *me*, just like I am about you...."

Blaze™

Dear Reader,

Some of you may have read *A Glimpse of Fire* with Dallas and Eric and *The Honeymoon That Wasn't* with Dakota and Tony. Dallas and Dakota are sisters, and in their books I sometimes mentioned their older brother, Cody. Frankly, I never planned on giving Cody his own book because I wasn't particularly fond of him in the beginning. He was too arrogant and not a guy I would personally want to hook up with. But being the oldest of three myself, I couldn't help but wonder and worry about him. Why hadn't he broken free from parental pressure as his sisters had? Work isn't everything. I didn't want his job or his parents to define him. He deserved happiness, too. I hope I gave it to him.

All my best,

Debbi Rawlins

IF HE ONLY KNEW...
Debbi Rawlins

HARLEQUIN®

TORONTO • NEW YORK • LONDON
AMSTERDAM • PARIS • SYDNEY • HAMBURG
STOCKHOLM • ATHENS • TOKYO • MILAN • MADRID
PRAGUE • WARSAW • BUDAPEST • AUCKLAND

ISBN-13: 978-0-373-79355-6
ISBN-10:   0-373-79355-3

IF HE ONLY KNEW...

ABOUT THE AUTHOR

Debbi Rawlins lives in central Utah, out in the country, surrounded by woods and deer and wild turkeys. It's quite a change for a city girl, who didn't even know where the state of Utah was until four years ago. Of course, unfamiliarity never stopped her. Between her junior and senior years of college she spontaneously left home in Hawaii, and bummed around Europe for five weeks by herself. And much to her parents' delight, returned home with only a quarter in her wallet.

Books by Debbi Rawlins

HARLEQUIN BLAZE

*Men To Do
**Do Not Disturb

Don't miss any of our special offers. Write to us at the following address for information on our newest releases.

Harlequin Reader Service
U.S.: 3010 Walden Ave., P.O. Box 1325, Buffalo, NY 14269
Canadian: P.O. Box 609, Fort Erie, Ont. L2A 5X3

Prologue

HEADS TURNED toward the door of Mist, the chic Manhattan bar where high-priced attorneys hung out after work and didn't mind paying twenty bucks for a peach martini. Brisk early-spring air rushed into the cozy burgundy-accented room, but that wasn't what commanded the attention of the tony crowd.

Sara Wells's heart started a slow, torturous pounding. She didn't have to look to know who'd just walked in. The last person she'd expect to come to her going-away party. Why would he? After all, she'd been a lowly temporary worker. Showing up wouldn't help his career or get him in tomorrow's society pages. And that was about all Cody Shea seemed to live for.

Even so, she'd foolishly wished with all her heart he'd show up. That she'd see him just one more time before she got on that plane tomorrow. God, but she wanted to look. Of course she wouldn't stoop to even the tiniest peek.

"I want you to know that if you change your mind, the job is still yours." Dakota, who'd been her boss until an hour ago, slid into a seat across from Sara at the small table.

"What? Oh, um, thanks." With incredible will-power, she kept her eyes away from the door and stared at the huge green concoction Dakota had set in front of her. Chunks of salt clung to the rim of the glass. "A margarita?"

"You haven't had a margarita until you've had one here."

Not that she'd tell Dakota, but in truth, she hadn't had a margarita. She stuck with wine. White, mostly. A glass with dinner since she was seventeen. But not during the last ten months she'd been living in New York. With rent being what it was, she hadn't been able to afford wine. Not the good stuff, anyway. And she'd rather drink tap water than cheap wine.

Dakota touched her hand, and Sara met her eyes. "I hope Cody isn't the reason you're leaving New York."

"No," she said truthfully. Her year of "dangerous" living was up. It was time to go home. She sighed. "Does everyone in the office know about my silly crush?"

"No, not even my idiotic brother." Her smile turned into a slight frown. "Although Cody has been acting pretty strange for the past couple of months." She gave a small shake of her head. "I told him some of us were coming here for a farewell drink, but I wouldn't count on him showing up."

Sara couldn't help it then. She turned her head slightly, enough to see Cody in his navy blue Alexander McQueen suit, standing at the black polished bar, listening to another attorney from the firm. Staring at her.

Their gazes collided. He didn't smile. Didn't look away. Just stared.

Dakota's gaze followed. "Well, I'll be damned."

Sara swung back around to face Dakota, her breathing obstructed by the growing lump in her throat. God, she didn't understand him one bit. Staring at her like that in front of everyone.

"Won't this be the topic of conversation in the office on Monday?" Dakota said, her gaze moving between Sara and her brother.

"Glad I won't be there." Sara's mouth was so dry the words almost didn't come out. She picked up the margarita and took a long cool sip. It was surprisingly good, and not just because she was parched.

Dakota's lips curved in a wry smile. "Sure you don't want to stay?"

Sara nodded. "Not that you haven't been the best boss ever."

"That could get you a raise." Dakota studied her for a moment. "You really should think about finishing law school. If tuition is a problem, the firm would—"

Sara shook her head, wanting to tell Dakota the truth. That she not only didn't need the money, but that she already had her law degree. That most people went to Europe when they graduated, footloose and fancy-free, but that Sara had chosen instead to come to New York and get a traditional job for traditional pay, just to see what it was like to be normal. To not be Sara Wellington, at least for a while. Of course, it didn't matter now. Tomorrow she'd be on the first flight back to Atlanta. Back to her real life. She supposed she could tell Dakota who she really was, but that would just invite a lot of questions, and frankly, answering them was the last thing she wanted to face at her going-away party.

"Okay, no pressure. I just wanted—" Dakota's smile widened as she looked past Sara. "Tony's here. I asked him to stop by."

"Good. I'd like to say goodbye." Sara looked over her shoulder. Cody was the first person she saw. Standing closer this time, talking to a paralegal two tables away.

He looked over at Sara and a slight smile lifted the corners of his mouth. She quickly turned away, suddenly warm and not so thrilled he'd come. What would it accomplish? Except to make her wish that they'd had a chance to get to know each other.

But then he would never allow that to happen. Careful about his image and personal life, Cody liked to keep himself removed from the rest of the staff. He was good at it, too. No one would think of approaching him unless it was work-related and absolutely necessary. People who'd worked with him for years didn't really know him.

Sara's perception of him had changed one night after hours when she'd overheard him talking to his secretary. The woman had been crying.

Sara's first reaction was outrage but as she listened she realized the tears had been in gratitude. Cody had spent his own money and time to track down her ex-husband and secure the woman's delinquent child support payments. His only condition was that the woman agree never to speak of it again.

After that, everything changed, at least in Sara's eyes. Too bad he never let others see that human side of him. Did he think it made him look weak?

Soft jazz filled the air, and Sara tried to focus on the soothing sound of the keyboard and not Cody. Socializing, talking to his subordinates. Being human. Reminding her of that night four months ago. Better to remember that than if they had hooked up, then leaving would be a hundred times more difficult than it already was.

"I don't think Tony sees us. I'll go get him." Dakota got up. "We'll be right back."

Sara nodded, and feeling her throat tighten again, picked up the margarita. The icy coldness soothed the inside of her mouth and the heat that had started in her chest. Now would be the perfect time for Cody to approach her.

The thought had barely crossed her mind when she felt him behind her. She forced herself to breathe as she pulled back her shoulders.

"Hey, Sara." Wrong voice. It was one of the junior attorneys from the firm who claimed Dakota's seat.

"Oh, Barry." What did he want? He'd hardly said a dozen words to her in the past six months.

He hesitated. "You expecting someone?"

"Dakota went to get her fiancé." Sara casually glanced over her shoulder, ostensibly to look for Dakota. Cody was gone. She twisted all the way around. No sign of him.

"I just wanted to buy you a drink."

Only a lifetime of Southern hospitality stopped her jaw from dropping to the table. "*You* want to buy me a drink?"

He looked a little sheepish and quickly turned to signal the waitress.

"Thanks, Barry, really, but this is going to be my last one."

"Look, I don't blame you for being ticked at me. I've been a jerk."

"I hadn't noticed."

With his caramel-colored eyes and dark hair he was good-looking when he smiled, but that didn't happen often. "Dakota told me about the screwup you caught on the Clarkson brief. I was pissed at first."

"Me being a temp and all."

"Well, yeah," he said unabashedly. "Then I heard you caught a mistake Margot made, too. Bottom line, you saved my ass."

Sara shrugged a shoulder. "Not a problem. I had to type it, so of course I noticed."

He shook his head. "You had to understand the content to notice. Most of the secretaries have been with the firm for years but couldn't have caught it on a dare. You're wasting your time. You should be in law school."

Sara just smiled. Been there. Done that. Yale. Second in her class. But none of these people needed to know that.

Barry studied her for a moment. "You have plans for dinner?"

"I have to pack. Early flight tomorrow."

"Where are you going again?"

"Atlanta," Cody answered for her.

Sara and Barry both stared as he pulled out a chair and joined them.

His knee brushed hers and the slight touch sent her pulse skittering. "Hope I'm not interrupting."

Barry looked from him to Sara and then back to Cody. "I didn't know you hung out here, boss."

"I don't."

After an awkward silence, Barry noisily cleared his throat. "Right." He pushed his chair back. "Okay, well, I guess I'll be going."

Cody didn't say anything, simply sipped from the glass he'd brought with him.

Barry stood. "Good luck to you, Sara. Travel safely."

She smiled, and then waited until Barry was out of earshot. "You were rude to him."

"Was I?" Cody's gaze narrowed and he seemed genuinely surprised.

"If you hadn't noticed, we're at a party. My party."

"That's why I'm here."

She watched him stop a passing waitress and order another scotch, shaking her head when he added a margarita. After the woman left, Sara asked, "Why do you do that?"

"Do what?"

"Treat people that way."

He frowned. "The waitress?"

"No, Barry. Other people in the office."

He leaned back in the burgundy leather club chair,

studying her, amusement in his eyes. "You make it sound like I'm an ogre."

Sara leaned forward, staying locked on his gaze. He didn't show surprise at her boldness, but she knew it was there. She'd purposely played the stereotypical Southern belle for the past ten months, sweet and accommodating. But she didn't have to play a part any longer.

Maintaining eye contact, she said, "Number one, you're aloof, which makes you inaccessible to your employees, and if you have a sense of humor, you hide it well. Does everything have to be all business all the time?"

It occurred to her in a flash of belated insight that she wasn't angry about how Cody treated Barry. She was pissed at how he'd treated her. Oh, he hadn't been mean or anything, but he had to have felt the sparks that ignited every time they were together. His being here was proof that she hadn't been the only one who'd been smitten. So why now? Why not months ago, when she could have done something about it?

The margarita beckoned as the truth hit her once again. He hadn't pursued her because he thought she was a secretary. A temporary one, at that.

She sipped her drink, her gaze turned away from his, wishing she had left ten minutes ago. Oh, hell. Who was she to judge Cody for being an arrogant snob? That he had sized her up by her appearance? She certainly wanted him based on his.

"That's it? That's the whole lecture?" The right corner of his mouth slowly lifted.

"Yep. That's the whole thing." She looked away, planning her exit strategy.

Instead of reaching for her purse, however, she made the mistake of looking at him. Dammit. He was doing it again. Staring at her with a hungry intensity that made her want to throw herself at him. It was that very look that had made the last few months such hell for her. That hunger had met her every time he'd come by her desk to drop off a motion or brief for Dakota. He'd lingered, never talking about anything but work and the weather, but the current had run between them, hotter than a live wire.

His secretary had done everything else for him, including getting his coffee and lunch and dry cleaning. So yes, every trip by her desk had been designed to torment and tease. Yet, he'd never taken the next step.

At first, she'd thought it was because they worked together, but the company had no policy about that. She'd found out that a couple of years ago, Cody had dated an attorney who'd since gone on to another firm. So the precedent had existed.

She simply hadn't met his standards.

The waitress brought his scotch, and he slipped her some money and told her to keep the change. The tip was a large one judging by the younger woman's eyes, but she didn't get a smile with it. Had he ever smiled in his life? Not the kind you gave the camera, or what was expected by a client, but a real spontaneous smile?

He adjusted his red silk tie and for a crazy second she thought he might loosen the knot. "You're a strange one, Sara Wells."

She blinked at him, confused. "Me? Why am I strange?"

"I can't put my finger on it, but something's... off."

"Pardon me?"

He chuckled, and at the odd sound coming from his mouth she almost slid off her chair. "I've known a lot of legal secretaries in my day, and none of them were like you."

"What were you expecting?"

He shook his head. "So illusive..." he said, but more to himself than her.

"Is that why you came tonight? For one last chance to get your answers?" she asked.

"Maybe. But mostly I came to say goodbye."

Her heart skidded at the quietness of his voice. "That happy to be rid of me, huh?"

His expression tightened. "No."

Uncomfortable, Sara glanced around. Dakota and Tony had sat at another table and they, along with everyone else from the office, seemed to be staring in Sara's direction.

This was nuts. None of this mattered. Not his voice, not his eyes, not even the reason that she dreamt about him night after night. Tomorrow she'd be gone.

She checked her watch, but it didn't matter what time it was. "I really need to get going. I have so much packing to do yet."

He didn't hide his surprise. "It's early."

"So is my flight tomorrow." She got up and grabbed her purse from where she'd left it on the chair beside her. "I'd better go say goodbye to Dakota and Tony."

"Wait."

She took a deep breath and turned back to him. The desire in his eyes totally unsettled her.

"You'll be coming back to New York sometime, won't you?"

"I doubt it."

"I see." He paused. "Well, you did a fine job for us. Thank you."

Absurdly disappointed, she smiled. "That's what you paid me for."

He nodded slowly, looking as if he had more to say.

"Goodbye, Mr. Shea."

Without looking back, she hurried over to Dakota, the one person in New York she'd truly miss. "Hey, Tony," she said, giving his shoulder a squeeze. "Good to see you."

"I don't blame you for ditching my brother," Dakota said, laughing, as Tony got to his feet. "Here, take my chair," he said. "I'll get another one."

"No." Sara shook her head and waved Tony back to his seat. "I have to go."

Dakota's eyebrows went up. "So soon?" And then her gaze drew to Cody. "Did he—?"

"I have an early flight. That's all." Sara smiled. It wasn't as if she'd be missed. She hadn't clicked with anyone other than Dakota. Not that Sara didn't appreciate people stopping by, but she also knew many of them frequented the bar on Fridays anyway. "I'll call you sometime, okay?"

"I'm counting on it." Dakota stood and gave her a warm hug. So did Tony. They were great together. Opposites in so many ways. And yet, they made it work. Probably because Dakota, unlike her brother, had taken the time to get to know him, just as she had gotten to know Sara, even though she was just a temporary secretary.

"Okay, I have to go before I start crying like an idiot." Unexpectedly, the tears had started to burn the back of her eyes, which was stupid because she'd known from the beginning she would be leaving now. Life here had gotten so much more complicated than she'd ever dreamed.

She briefly waved to everyone scattered around the bar, careful not to look at Cody, then rushed to the door. Her heated cheeks welcomed the crisp air and she didn't care that she had no coat, just her tweed suit jacket.

Two cabs on the corner both had passengers and no others were in sight, so she started walking toward Lexington. The light turned red and she slowed down, wrapping her arms around herself. A huge chapter in her life had just ended. An unsatisfying chapter. Not just because being normal hadn't been all she'd dreamed it would be, but mostly because of Cody.

"Sara…wait."

Had she imagined his voice? She looked over her shoulder. Cody hurried toward her, his shoulders hunched against the chill, his hands in his pockets. She couldn't have moved if she'd wanted to. His gaze held her rooted to the spot even as pedestrians swirled around her.

He caught up with her and, taking her by the arm, steered her out of the way toward the bank that took up most of the block. Partially sheltered from the sharp wind that whipped through the canyon of high-rises, she shrunk closer to the gray brick building as she tamped down her foolish hope.

"Did I forget something?" she asked, breathless, annoyed that his face was in shadow.

"No, I did." He pulled a small Tiffany box out of his pants' pocket and held it out to her.

"What is it?"

"Open it."

"But I—" Her heart pounded so hard he had to be able to hear it. All of Manhattan could. "Is this from you?"

He glanced around and pushed a hand through his short, sandy-brown hair. "From the firm. For doing such a good job."

"Really?" She took the box, her hand shaking a little because she knew he was lying and it made her angry. Couldn't he be candid for one moment? Not even on her last night in New York?

"Aren't you going to open it?" he asked when she slipped it into her bag.

"Later."

He exhaled loudly, cursed, then took a step closer. "It's from me."

The smile began in the pit of her stomach and how it managed to pass through the tightness in her chest, she couldn't imagine. She should be angry. Furious. He was too late. Whatever was in the box would change nothing. Her time was up. She had to go back to Atlanta.

"Aren't you going to open it?"

She slid her arms around his neck and got up on tiptoe. "This is from me," she whispered and brought her mouth to his, running her tongue across his lower lip.

His arms came around her and he pulled her against him. He plunged his tongue inside her mouth with passion. She kissed him back with equal intensity even though tears threatened.

Damn him.

She pulled away and was lucky enough to hail a taxi.

She slid inside and wouldn't look back. What was the point? He'd blown their chance. She'd never see him again.

1

THE CHIC SALON was still decorated in its signature rose color, each workstation large and private. An abundance of fresh flowers graced the lobby and lounge where juice, Evian and wine were served to the prominent and wealthy clients while they donned silk robes and waited for their grooming services. Not a thing had changed in a year. Only Sara.

"Girl, I don't know what that guy did to you."

Sara lifted her horrified gaze to her hairdresser's reflection in the mirror. How could Chloe possibly know about Cody? No one knew. Except Sara's sister. And the ladies from Eve's Apple, the Web site where women went to vent or ask advice about men, anonymously if they chose.

"I could've given you a better cut with my eyes closed."

Sara relaxed. As much as she could. Her nerves were shot from lack of sleep. She'd only been back in Atlanta for a month, but with all the family obligations it seemed like a year.

"I can't believe you've been walking around like this. You should've come to see me as soon as you got back." Chloe's hair was red this month, her green eyes rimmed with too much black. "Everybody makes a big deal out of New York and L.A. hairdressers. They treat them like frackin' gurus." She held up a thick blond lock of Sara's hair and frowned at the dry ends. "How much did you pay for this highlighting?"

"None of your business."

"Come on."

Her experience in New York hadn't lived up to her expectations. In fact, it'd gone bad. All she'd wanted was to live like anyone else. Earn her keep. What she hadn't counted on was meeting Cody Shea, and having her life turned upside down. She thought about him way too much as it was, she had no desire to talk about it, not even with Chloe. "Would you forget it, already?"

"How many years have I been doing your hair? How many boyfriends have we gone through together?"

Sara raised her eyebrows.

"Okay, so they were all mine. The point is, I tell you everything."

"Yes, you do. Whether I want to hear it or not."

Chloe grinned. "Speaking of which, guess where I'm going tonight?" She paused, and before Sara could hazard a guess, she said, "The French Riviera."

"Just for the weekend?"

"No, for a whole week. It's our annual convention."

"Are we talking hairdressers or nudists?"

"Please." Chloe set the mixed color solution aside and got out the foil squares. "Like I'd fork out that much money to spend the week with a bunch of prima donnas who think they know more about hair than I do."

"Of course not." Smiling, Sara watched her strategically choose strands to highlight and then clip them off to the side.

In the ten years that Sara had known Chloe, she'd gone from a cosmetology graduate to one of Atlanta's most popular and expensive hairstylists. Admittedly, discovering that Chloe was a nudist had been somewhat of a surprise. Sara couldn't grasp the attraction. Running around naked, in the stark sunlight, every flaw on full display. The thought alone gave her the vapors.

"Shelby still in Europe?"

"Last I heard. But you know how my sister is."

"I haven't read about her in the local papers lately so I figured she was still out of town. Hey, is that a new bracelet?"

Sara automatically touched the row of abstract gold hearts, unwanted memories filling her head. Stupid to even wear the thing, but she hadn't taken it off since that night. "I got it in New York."

"But you hate bracelets. You don't even like wearing a watch."

"Don't go too light," Sara said, eyeing the bowl of color solution Chloe had dipped the brush in and started to work on the pre-selected strands.

"You're a natural blonde. How light can I go?"

Chloe said, as she wrapped a square of foil around the strand.

Sara said nothing. All she'd really wanted to do was distract Chloe from the bracelet. She glanced down at it. Were those really hearts or was that what she wanted to see? She'd browsed in Tiffany's often, and even had several of the store's signature gifts given to her tucked away in her drawers, but she'd never seen this style.

"You gonna get that?" Chloe nudged her chin toward the cell phone Sara had left on the counter. The ringing cell phone.

She'd been expecting an important call from her father and grabbed the phone before the call went to voice mail. The second she pushed the button she saw that the call was from New York. Too late. She had to answer. Anyway, it could be Dakota. "Hello?"

"Sara."

Except that it was Cody. Her throat constricted. For a second she couldn't speak.

"Sara?"

"Yes." She looked at Chloe who was staring at her with curiosity. "Um, could you hold on a moment?" She lowered the phone to her side so that he couldn't hear and struggled to her feet, getting tangled in the cape and tugging it from around her neck.

Brush in midair, Chloe backed out of her way. "What are you doing?"

"I'll be right back."

"Where are you going?"

Sara didn't answer. Nor did she acknowledge the

stares of the other clients as she hurried through the salon in the pink silk robe and with packets of foil wrapped in her hair. She went past the reception desk and straight out into the street before bringing the phone to her ear again.

"Sorry," she said, trying to blend into the landscaped courtyard beside the entrance.

"Is this a bad time?" His deep voice went right through her, taking her back to that night. That kiss.

"No, not really. I'm just surprised to hear from you." She figured Dakota might have called, but never Cody.

"Are you?"

"What?"

"Really surprised?"

"Yes. Really." She turned her back to a couple strolling by on the sidewalk. When a teenage boy riding a skateboard slowed down near her to stare, she glared at him. "What?"

"I beg your pardon?" Cody asked uncertainly.

"No, not you. It was this kid—"

"This is a bad time."

"No, I mean—is there anything in particular you wanted?" That came out totally wrong. She should've sent him a thank-you note for the bracelet. She'd even made several attempts. But in the end, cowardice won over manners.

After a long pause, he said, "How about I call you back later?"

"No, it's okay. Anyway, I wanted to thank you for the bracelet." The breathless words were barely out of her mouth when she heard the salon door open and turned to see Chloe frowning at her.

"You realize you can exchange it if you don't like it."

She gave Chloe her back and lowered her voice. "Oh, no, I love it. I'm wearing it right now, in fact."

"Good." He sounded genuinely pleased. "Look, the reason I called is to ask if you'd have dinner with me."

"Dinner?" Was he kidding? "When?"

"Tonight."

"But—" In the background, she heard a woman's voice announcing that a flight to Acapulco had been delayed. "Where are you?"

"Here. Atlanta."

She nearly dropped the phone.

"What's going on?" Chloe got in her face.

Sara fiercely waved her away while putting distance between them. "Are you at the airport?"

"I just arrived."

She swallowed. He hadn't wasted any time calling her. Should she be flattered, or scared out of her mind?

Scared won.

The truth wasn't her friend at the moment. She wasn't who Cody thought she was, and she wanted it left that way. She cleared her throat, then asked, "Here on business?"

"Yes, for the week."

That wasn't the answer she'd expected. When she'd worked for the firm, Cody never traveled. He'd always sent an underling. "Must be a big client."

"Yeah," he murmured. "About tonight?"

Cody. Here in Atlanta. It didn't seem real. "All right," she said slowly, trying to remember if she was supposed to be somewhere tonight. But she couldn't think straight. Not that it mattered. How could she not see him? "Where are you staying?"

"The Ritz-Carlton on Peachtree. Would you like to meet there?"

"No." She squeezed her eyes shut, mentally kicking herself for her abruptness. But she couldn't get through the lobby without a dozen people recognizing her. "I thought maybe you'd like to experience a little local color."

"Sure. Name the place."

Oh, God. "Could you hold for just a moment, please?" Without waiting for his answer, she turned to get Chloe. She was at the door of the salon about to go inside. Sara frantically motioned her back, and then met her halfway, holding the phone behind her back. "I need a name and address of a restaurant."

Chloe narrowed her gaze. "Is this a joke?"

"Chloe, please."

She gave Sara a curious look, and then said, "Café Tu Tu Tango in Buckhead."

"Thanks, I'll be right back in." She waited, keeping the phone right where it was so he couldn't hear.

Chloe gave her another questioning look and then went into the salon.

Sara brought the phone back up to her ear as the name Chloe had given her registered. Chloe wouldn't send her to someplace too weird, would she?

Ignoring the older woman with the ridiculously permed hair and disapproving look who climbed into the rear seat of a limo, Sara turned her attention back to Cody. "How about we meet at Café Tu Tu Tango in Buckhead? Any taxi driver will know where it is." Not that she did. Of course, she'd been to the Buckhead district many times, but not that restaurant.

"Fine. What time?"

She glanced at her watch. God, she was insane for doing this. "Seven-thirty?"

"I'll be there."

"Okay, me, too." She cringed at her lameness.

"I'm looking forward to seeing you, Sara," he said, his voice so low and husky her mouth went dry. Then he disconnected the call, leaving her weak-kneed and questioning the prudence of showing up tonight.

Of course she would. She had better manners than to stand anyone up. Oh, God. Where was Shelby when she needed her? Sara took a deep breath and headed back into the salon to face the stares and exchanged looks as she passed through the lobby. She ignored them all as she nonchalantly lowered herself back into Chloe's chair.

Chloe didn't miss a beat. She draped the cape Sara had discarded, then picked up the bowl of color solution. After glancing around, Chloe leaned close to Sara's ear. "What the hell is going on?"

"Nothing."

"Yeah, that's what I figured."

Sara disregarded the sarcasm. This wasn't

something she'd discuss with Chloe, especially since the woman's answer for everything was to go for it. Besides, Chloe didn't understand what it meant to be rich. She was like so many other people who thought money solved every problem. How could you be unhappy if you could buy anything you wanted?

Fortunately, they hadn't been defined by a trust fund, like Sara and her sister. As soon as a man heard Sara's last name, it was over. There was no way to tell if it was her he wanted. Or the money. Or the publicity. Those people who thought she had it so good hadn't had expectations so huge they thought they would choke on them. One mistake and the local press was all over them, almost as if they'd been waiting for one of the Wellingtons to fall from grace. There was no privacy. Not in Atlanta, anyway.

And here Cody was. In the thick of things. What was he doing here for an entire week? It didn't make sense. At least she knew where he was staying. She could call and excuse herself for tonight. Tell him she'd forgotten an engagement on her calendar.

In fact, now she had his cell number. Her gaze fell to the small cell phone she still clutched in her hand. Should she program his number, or…

"Fine. Give me the silent treatment." Chloe turned to sip her French vanilla latte and then with an acerbic look returned to brushing on the highlights.

Sara wasn't big on sharing confidences. Except, of course, with Shelby. Although she didn't have to worry about Chloe. She was discreet, just like every other stylist at Papillon in deference to their high-profile clientele.

"Okay, there was this guy in New York…"

"Yeah?" Chloe's eyebrows went up but she kept working. "And?"

"He didn't step up to the plate until my last night there. So honest, nothing to tell."

Stepping back, Chloe gave her a wry look.

"I'm serious."

"He give you the bracelet?"

"Yes, but nothing happened. He was…out of reach, you know?"

"If I didn't know better, I'd think you were high. The only man that could be out of reach for you is damn Prince Charles, but that's not the point. When was the last time you had a date?"

"I can always count on you to make me feel better."

"Sorry." Chloe smiled sheepishly. "Tell me about this guy and I promise to skip the editorials."

She breathed in deeply. "He's an attorney, a senior partner in one of the foremost law firms in Manhattan. But I think he's only about thirty-five. Which means he's intelligent and ambitious."

"Or that he's sleeping with the boss." Chloe winced, when Sara gave her a dirty look. "I'm supposed to shut up."

"That's what I get for asking the impossible."

"No, come on. What does he look like?"

"Tall, maybe just over six feet. Athletic-looking. Kind of light brown hair, or maybe you'd call it dark blond. I'm not sure what the difference is." She stopped and thought a moment. He wore his hair too short, in her opinion, so she really hadn't noticed it much. It was his eyes that got to her. "Bluish green," she said and then looked at an obviously confused Chloe. "His eyes. They're this bluish green color that's really hard to describe."

Chloe smiled and kept working.

"What?"

"Girl, you got it bad."

"I do not. He's just—" She slumped. "Okay, so what do I do about it?"

"You have to ask?"

"Ouch!" Sara jerked.

Chloe eased up on the hair she was applying color to. "That wasn't deliberate. Although I hope it jarred some sense into you."

"All right, all right. He's here for a week. I promise to see him at least twice."

Chloe sighed dramatically. "I'm so proud."

"I have one little problem." Sara met her eyes and waited for her words to sink in.

"He doesn't know who you are," Chloe said quietly.

Sara shook her head. "Which means I can't take him back to Shelby's and my apartment. And he's staying at the Ritz-Carlton."

"Shit."

"Couldn't have put it better myself."

"Wait." Chloe freed her hands and pulled out the top drawer. She withdrew a ridiculously small red purse and dug inside until she produced a set of keys. "Ta da. The answer is my apartment. Think about it.

The timing is perfect." Careful of her long red fingernails, she separated a key from the others and handed it to Sara. "I'll be gone for a week. I have to be at the airport tonight at six, so it's yours from 4 p.m. on."

Sara stared at the silver key in her hand. Was this fate, or what?

Chloe went back to work as if the matter were settled. "The microwave died a couple of months ago. I don't eat at home much, so I haven't replaced it. I don't even know if the oven works. But I've only had the apartment for two years."

Sara laughed. "You're sure about this? Because I can—"

"Come on, you wanna get laid, or what?"

Sara briefly closed her eyes. Not a good day for Chloe to be testing her patience.

"Relax. Nobody heard."

"Look, Chloe, I appreciate what you're doing, but you can't tell anyone about this. I'm serious."

"That hurt."

"I apologize." Sara sighed. This whole thing was too bizarre for words. "I do. I totally trust you."

"You gotta lighten up. You're only twenty-seven. Have some fun."

Technically Sara was still twenty-six, but darn it, Chloe was absolutely right. For the rest of her life she'd regret not jumping at this chance to be with Cody. She only wished the opportunity had presented itself in New York and not Atlanta where she knew half the people in the city. Or rather, they knew her.

2

At SEVEN-FIFTEEN, Cody slowly got out of the cab in front of Café Tu Tu Tango. He knew this was the right restaurant. Unlikely he'd have gotten both the name and location wrong, and the driver had known exactly where to go. But this definitely wasn't the type of restaurant he'd had in mind. Nor would he have guessed it was the kind of place that met with Sara's taste.

But then again, what did he really know about the woman? Other than she couldn't be more wrong for him and had a wide smile that made him behave like a stupid prepubescent teen. In his saner moments he'd wondered about her many contradictions. She'd sublet a fifth-floor walk-up in Manhattan that was the size of a postage stamp, and she didn't go with the rest of the staff to their daily lunches, preferring to eat alone in the park or at her desk from the same brown paper bag. Yet she wore really expensive shoes and, according to his sources, her purse cost a bundle, and it wasn't a knockoff.

Nothing wrong with desiring the finer things. He settled for nothing less. But he knew how much money she made as a temporary office worker. Something didn't add up. And that should have made him nervous. Not intrigued.

In fact, he almost hoped that he'd find out she was one of *those* women. The kind that lived in dives and spent all their money on expensive accessories and hung out at ritzy bars in the hope of finding a rich husband.

A couple of law school friends had been taken to the cleaners by women of that ilk, but he'd been lucky to avoid the trap himself. Actually, luck had nothing to do with it. He was careful. Selective. Although he had no political ambitions at this point, he had no intention of screwing up his career or any future options.

He looked again at the colorful restaurant sign. Café Tu Tu Tango? Maybe it was a Southern thing.

Taking a deep breath, he looked at his watch. One week. That's all he'd be in Atlanta for. He'd probably have dinner with Sara a couple of times. Maybe even invite her back to his hotel for one discreet night. Then he'd head back to New York. How much trouble could he get into?

He headed for the door of the restaurant, his step quickening at the thought of seeing Sara. If he didn't like the place, he'd persuade her to come back to the hotel with him, to the Atlanta Grill.

Just as he opened the door, a couple stumbled out. He quickly moved back, but the woman's stiff blue spiked hair scraped across his chin, the heavy smell of gin assaulting his nostrils.

"'Scuse us," the young man with an unfortunate tattoo scrawled around his neck said, and then guided his partner down the sidewalk.

Cody adjusted his right cuff. This obviously was not a good idea. Stepping inside the restaurant further convinced him. Not only was the place packed with people, but the room itself was a dizzying avalanche of color. And noise. God almighty.

There were paintings everywhere, on practically every surface. Everything from contemporary oils to copies of masterpieces. There was a rather loud three-piece band on a second-story stage, and dancers with big blue twirling skirts.

"Hi, do you have a reservation?" A pretty blonde, or she might have been had she not had both her nose and left eyebrow pierced and bolted, approached him.

"I don't think so." He glanced around, hoping Sara had also arrived early.

"Oops." Sighing, the blonde consulted a list, using the tip of a bright pink fingernail that matched her short tight spandex dress. "We're full up tonight."

"Thank you, anyway." He'd wait outside and give Sara the *bad* news. Meanwhile, he'd get them another reservation.

"Were you meeting someone?"

He'd already started to leave and withdrawn his cell phone to call the hotel concierge. "Yes, but that's all right."

"What's the name?"

"Sara Wells."

"Ah, yes. Chloe made a reservation for the two of you. The lady's not here yet, though." The woman smiled, and Cody caught a flash of a silver stud embedded in her tongue. "You can wait at the table or the bar."

Damn. He jammed his cell phone back inside his suit jacket. "The table, thank you." He glanced over his shoulder toward the door, futilely hoping to see Sara, and then followed the blonde to a table in the back of the restaurant.

Although the patrons were an odd assortment of yuppies and bohemian types, none appeared to be financially lacking. Judging by the abundance of Louis Vuitton and Chanel purses sitting on tables, and the gold Rolexes encircling many a wrist. Of course the accessories could all be knockoffs, or then again, supporting evidence of social climbing.

God, he didn't want to think that about Sara. But he wasn't going to be taken for a fool, either.

He sat down, taking the seat that faced the entry, and was promptly approached by a waitress who took his scotch order. While he waited, he glanced around and noticed that a young man was actually painting on a canvas while three others at his table watched. The abstract he worked on was actually pretty good. He couldn't say the same for the acoustics. The music was too loud, and so was the laughter and chatter all around him. He'd wanted a nice, quiet dinner. One where he and Sara could talk.

The waitress returned with his drink, but before he could ask her anything, he saw Sara heading toward him. A simple, sleeveless cream-colored blouse was tucked into the slim waist of her jeans, and her blond hair seemed slightly wilder than he remembered her wearing it. Longer, too, skimming her shoulders. She looked so beautiful.

He started to rise but she waved for him to stay seated. To his amazement, his heart beat faster the closer she got to him. That hadn't happened since he was twenty. In court, at times, while awaiting a verdict. But he hadn't been this attracted to a woman since...

Since that damn kiss.

"Traffic was brutal," she said as she pulled out a chair and gracefully sat down. "I hope you haven't been waiting long."

"Just got here. And I'm early." He'd forgotten how much he liked her lilting Southern accent. Not too pronounced. Soothing. Which was odd, because accents generally annoyed him.

She glanced at her watch, frowned and then promptly lowered her wrist and smiled. "Interesting place, huh?"

"That's an understatement."

She looked past him, her gaze narrowing as it flitted around.

"It's got a lot of energy." He caught their waitress's eye as she served drinks at another table and she gave him a nod.

"I'll say."

"You seem surprised."

She shifted, clearly uncomfortable, but only

shrugged a shoulder. "I was getting my hair done when you called and I asked my hairdresser for a recommendation."

"Ah. I like it."

"What?"

"Your hair."

"Oh." She absently tugged at a curl that wound its way toward her cheek. "Not my usual."

"No," he agreed. At work she'd always worn her hair in a sleeker style, one he normally preferred on women. But this sexy tousled look suited her heart-shaped face and contradicted those clear, innocent blue eyes. "So where do you usually go?"

"Me?"

He smiled. "Yes."

Sara gave a self-deprecating shake of her head, her lips curving. "I don't go out much."

He found that hard to believe. She had to have a lot of dates. "Really?"

She briefly met his eyes and then turned her attention to the waitress who'd finally shown up. Sara ordered white wine, and then changed her mind and asked for a frozen margarita. "Dakota got me hooked on those," she said as the waitress walked away. "How is she, by the way?"

"Great. Busy as usual."

Sara's gaze narrowed. "So what are you doing in Atlanta?"

"Representing a client."

"I didn't think you ever left New York."

He smiled. Basically, that was true.

"Seriously. I would've thought you'd have sent Matthew or Sterling."

"Yes, well…" Of course he should have. Everyone in the office was probably wondering the same thing. Dakota had been the only one to call him on his decision to come himself. She'd even had the nerve to ask if Sara was the reason. As if he'd let his personal feelings influence a professional decision. "The guy I'm representing…his father is an important client and he's called in a favor. His son's gotten himself into a little trouble that's become too public."

She seemed to tense, her pink-tinted lips tightening as she leaned forward. "Anyone I would know?"

The local papers had already run the story so it wasn't a matter of maintaining confidentiality. Her reaction, however, made him hesitate. He shook it off. What difference could it possibly make? "Harrison Manning Junior."

"Ah." She relaxed back in her chair. "I read something about him in the newspaper. He'll never see the inside of a courtroom."

"Not if I do my job," he said, confused at the flash of anger in her eyes. "Do you know him?"

"He's in the *Journal* a lot. This isn't the first time he's gotten himself in a mess."

That was news to him. "Really?" Cody picked up his drink and took a sip while studying her over the rim, his curiosity piqued. This was supposed to be a slam dunk case.

She blushed a pretty pink, then shook her head. "I don't really know. It's just gossip."

He decided he didn't want to talk about Harrison Manning Junior. "What have you been doing?" he asked. "Since you got back."

She looked down at her hands, then back at him. "Still temping."

That surprised and annoyed him. She was too talented to still be drifting. "Dakota tells me you've taken some law classes…"

She nodded and then picked up one of the menus the hostess had left. "Have you had a look at this, yet?"

"She also told me that you'd caught a couple of significant errors in—"

She looked up, clearly flustered. "Are you trying to recruit me?"

"I thought I was making small talk."

Sighing, she sank back. "Sorry. I had a bad day. Traffic. You know…"

"Well, since you brought it up, how would you like to assist me while I'm here? Thirty percent over whatever we paid you in New York."

Her gaze met his, her blue eyes narrowing in alarm. Her lips, pink and glistening from a slow swipe of her tongue, parted slightly. "I already have a job this week."

"Hey, that's fine. That's good. Just thought I'd…" He picked up his menu and pretended to read it. He had to stop staring at Sara before he said or did something stupid again. What if she'd accepted his ridiculous offer? Where had that come from, anyway? He'd always kept his social and professional life separate.

That was the problem. He didn't know what he wanted from Sara. His whole attraction to her was weird. Sure she was gorgeous, but they basically had nothing in common. It wasn't like college, where he felt free to pursue any woman at any time. Besides the fact that he wasn't a kid anymore, his career was too important for him to not be discriminating.

"Cody, what are you really doing here?" she asked, breaking into his thoughts, her tone bordering on accusing, as if she'd read his mind.

He reluctantly looked up from the menu. "Excuse me?"

"Come on. Tell me."

The challenge in her eyes made him smile. "I have a client—"

She tilted her head to the side. "I know why you're here. I just don't understand it."

"Don't understand what?"

"You barely gave me the time of day when I was in New York."

"That's not true."

"And then that last night—" She briefly looked away, and then stared back with determination, leaning closer, the undersides of her breasts grazing the table. In a low voice, she asked, "What was that about?"

He felt his face flush in embarrassment. He turned to his menu and prayed for a waitress.

"Don't be defensive. Please. I just don't understand why you didn't ask me out months ago."

He looked up at the change in her tone. There was

no accusation, just curiosity, and that he understood. "You were working for the firm."

She looked him straight in the eyes. "Was that the only reason?"

He shook his head. "Man, I should've gone to a Braves' game."

"I assume that means I'm not going to get any more out of you, right? Well, that's okay. I shouldn't have put you on the spot. As for the Braves, they're out of town, playing the Cubs. But they'll be back on Wednesday."

"You like baseball?"

Her eyes widened. "Doesn't everyone?"

"Uh, no. You go to the games?"

"Most of them. Are you a Mets' fan by any chance?"

Amazing. She was the only woman he knew who liked baseball. "Hell, yes."

"I bet you have great season tickets."

"I don't have time to go to the games. I try to catch the scores on ESPN."

"That's sad," she said earnestly. "The fun part of baseball is sitting in the stadium with all the noise and eating hot dogs and popcorn. Oh, and I love those big pretzels."

He smiled at the rapture on her face, at the flash of memory from his college days. Before law school. Before life had gotten so damn complicated. "Don't forget a tall frosty beer."

She wrinkled her nose. "I can do without that."

"Normally, I'd agree. But there's something about a ball park dog and a cold beer that can't be beat."

Her lips curved in a mysterious smile before she obstructed it by taking a sip of her margarita.

The odd smile and her silence made his eyes narrow. "You know something I don't?"

"Probably a lot of things." Salt from the rim of the glass clung to her lower lip and she used the tip of her tongue to remove the small chunk. Slowly, as if she knew the act was driving him crazy.

He silently cleared his throat. "Is that right?"

She nodded, and then she went real still, staring at him as if she'd just now realized he was at the table. To say the look was unnerving was an understatement.

"What are you doing tomorrow night for dinner?" she asked.

The way she asked matched the gleam in her eyes, and he wasn't sure if he should be thrilled or head back to New York on the next flight. "Why?"

"Here's the thing." She placed her clasped hands on the table and leaned forward with no hint of a smile. "This is my territory."

"Meaning?"

"If you want to see me, it'll be on my terms."

Cody snorted. Who did she think she was talking to? He could have a date every night of the week if he wanted. With attractive Manhattan socialites. Prominent career women. Sara was a damn temp worker, and she thought she could dictate terms to him?

He drained his scotch. "What?" he asked, as he realized with a jolt that her terms might be very, very interesting. "What are your terms?"

"First, we'll only—"

"Shelby?" A tall, balding man, wearing a well-tailored suit, approached the table. "I thought you were still in Europe."

She blinked and her face paled. "Robert?" She shot out of her chair, glanced at Cody and said, "Would you excuse me?" before taking the man's arm and steering him toward the front of the restaurant.

Cody watched until he couldn't see her anymore, and then stared at the amber liquid at the bottom of his tumbler. Barely a taste of scotch remained. The man had called her Shelby, and she obviously knew him. She hadn't been in Europe. She'd been living in New York. What the hell was going on?

Their waitress was taking orders at the next table, and Cody couldn't decide if he should get another drink or disappear before Sara got back. What did he know about the woman, anyway?

Using a different name. Lying about going to Europe. Choosing a restaurant she'd never been to before.

It all spelled trouble.

He reached into his jacket for his wallet, anxious to pay his tab and get out, when he saw her heading back toward him, without the balding man. Long blond tendrils bounced as she walked and even from three table lengths away, he could see the sapphire blue of her eyes. But it was the slow wide smile and straight white teeth that got him. Right in the gut. And lower.

"Sorry," she said in a breathy voice as she sat

down. Her gaze briefly scanned the room behind him, before she met his eyes.

"What was that about?"

"He's a family friend," she said without blinking, without displaying any other sign she was lying.

"But he doesn't know your name?"

Her eyebrows went up in challenge. "He mistook me for my sister."

"Right."

"Okay, here's the deal." She reached behind for the black leather purse she'd hung on the chair back. "As I said, my territory, my terms. This is nonnegotiable. I choose where we go, what we do. I'm leaving now. If you can deal with that, come with me. Otherwise, the best of luck on your case."

He needed at least one more scotch. "Are you serious?"

She'd already gotten up and stopped only to give him a definitive nod before walking away.

Screw her. The woman was totally insane. His gaze stayed on the graceful sway of her slim hips, the way her jeans hugged the generous swell of her backside. Instead of getting his questions answered, he had a dozen more. She wasn't just intriguing, she was infuriating. He should be grateful to get out of this so easily.

Shit.

He threw a couple of twenties on the table and then hurried after her.

3

SARA LOOKED straight ahead until she got out of the restaurant and into the chilled evening air. She should have known better. Did she think she could get away with going to a restaurant in Buckhead and not seeing someone she knew? She'd have been better off choosing a place out of the phone book. Someplace on the far side of town. Not that it mattered now. From the look on Cody's face, she knew she'd never see him again. Which was probably just as well.

Damn him. Why hadn't he made a move in New York? All that time wasted…

She jerked open her purse, looking for her car keys and then remembered she'd taken a cab. Since taxis weren't abundant in the area, she'd have to call for one. Sighing, she got out her cell phone while glancing up at the darkening sky. Looked like rain. Great.

She sensed him behind her a moment before he laid a warm hand on her bare arm. Sucking in a breath, she slowly looked up at him. His eyes were more green than blue and the surprising hint of stubble on his chin made him look more rugged than usual. As quick as that, she knew she'd been full of it, thinking his loss was no big deal.

"Okay," he said simply. "You win."

"It's not a matter of winning or losing. It's just—" A chill chased up her spine and she shivered.

He moved closer and slid an arm around her shoulders, bringing her against the warmth of his body. "Is this allowed?" he whispered.

The urge to give him a good shove faded next to the pleasure of being pressed against his chest. "Only because it's freezing out here."

He smiled. "Freezing?"

Sara sighed. So it was only in the low seventies. Still, it was unseasonably cool. And his chest felt so damn good. A lot stronger and more sculpted than she'd imagined. Despite his busy schedule, he obviously found time to work out. "We're going to have to take a taxi."

"You don't have a car?"

"I do, but it's in the shop."

He gave her an odd look, though there was no way he could know she'd lied. "No problem." Frowning, he looked down the street. But of course there were no taxis.

"This isn't like New York," she said. "Most people around here drive, so we'll have to call for a cab."

"Right." With a look of exasperation, he removed his arm from around her shoulders and reached into his breast pocket for his cell phone.

Immediately, she missed his touch. But the sudden realization that she had no idea where they should go next sent her thoughts in a different direction. There were a dozen places that she favored but none without consequence. Of course there was always Chloe's place. But the first night? Not a good idea.

"You wouldn't happen to know the number?"

She shook her head. "I'll run back inside and ask the hostess to call."

Before she could move, he took her hand. "I'll take care of it."

She didn't argue. She simply enjoyed the feel of his palm pressed to hers, the way his long fingers curled around her hand as he called directory assistance, even though the problem of where she'd take him once the cab arrived remained unsolved.

Was she being too cautious? At this point, did it really matter if he knew who she was? While living in New York, it hadn't just been about the anonymity. She'd genuinely wanted to know how it felt to live by herself, to depend on no one else for money or influence or anything else.

But now she was back to reality. And Cody would be here for one short week. He'd actually called and wanted to see her. Only for sex, of course. And only because he was here in Atlanta, where no one knew him. She laughed at the irony. Except it wasn't really funny. She still didn't know what to do. After all, what if he was *the one?*

The sudden ridiculous thought took her by surprise and erected her defenses so fast it made her chest tighten. She withdrew her hand from his and moved away, keeping her gaze averted. There could be nothing between them but sex. Anything more, for her especially, was out of the question.

"Are you all right?"

She looked over at him. He'd already put his cell phone away. Who knows how long he'd been watching her? "Did you get a hold of a cab?"

He hesitated, and she braced herself for an unwanted question. But all he said was, "One should be here within five minutes."

"Good." She checked her watch. Mostly for the distraction. She'd purposely not worn the bracelet. She didn't want him reading too much into it.

"Care to tell me where we're going?"

This time she did the stalling. Should she wing it? Get to the other side of town and then blindly choose a place at which to stop. Or should she play it safe and take him to Chloe's?

Safe? She nearly laughed out loud. There were so many questions in his gorgeous eyes, but there was also that spark, the connection she'd never thought she'd feel again.

All right. There was safe, and then there was safe.

She smiled up at him. "How about we go to my place?"

SARA NEEDN'T HAVE opened the door to Chloe's apartment to realize how incredibly dumb it was to have brought him here without having checked out the place first. Chloe was a terrific hairstylist but she was rather odd.

So was her taste in decorating. And that was putting it kindly.

As much as Sara wanted to block Cody's view, she knew there was no turning back now. Not without making him think she was nuts. There was nothing to do but plunge ahead and try not to cringe.

Taking a deep breath, she led Cody into the rather vibrant front room. Orange wasn't the color Sara would have chosen for the walls but there it was, an interesting contrast to the oversized lemon-yellow sofa that curved like a snake halfway around the freestanding fireplace.

Dreading it, she turned to look at Cody. She had to hand it to him, he kept a straight face. Of course, good lawyers could do that, and he was one of the best in the country.

She steered them farther into the room, and out of the corner of her eye, she caught sight of the small but open kitchen. Thankfully, she eyed a hutch near the glass dining table stocked with several bottles of booze. Premium stuff, which didn't surprise her. Chloe was truly gifted and commanded a hefty fee for her work. And she did enjoy the finer things. Even her furnishings, although on the bohemian side, looked like the highest quality.

"I see you like the retro look," Cody said, eyeing the lime-green side chairs with amused interest.

Sara paused, taking a new look at the place. It was retro, which, for whatever reason, seemed to make it less tacky. "Not really. I have a roommate. This was originally her place. I just moved in two weeks ago."

"Ah." He looked relieved.

She hid a smile and dropped her purse on a black lacquered console table beside a sculpture of a nude couple embracing.

Cody came up beside her and studied the sculpture. "Is she going to show up at any moment?"

"No, she's on her way to Europe."

His head reared back slightly. "Is that some kind of code?"

"Excuse me?"

"Didn't you say your sister—"

Sara laughed. "Yes, she really is in Europe. And Chloe left for the French Riviera—" she glanced at her watch "—about three hours ago."

"Quite a jet-setting crowd you hang around with."

"Chloe's also my hairdresser and with what she charges for a haircut, she could probably retire."

He didn't comment, just continued to check out the odd pieces of art that adorned the walls, the knickknacks of wrought-iron stick people holding silk flowers and glass fuchsia-colored high heels filled with colored marbles scattered about.

"Why don't you fix yourself a drink?" she suggested, trying to divert his attention so she could check out the rest of the apartment in privacy. "I'll be right back."

"All right," he said, turning to look at her. Their eyes met and his crinkled with humor. "Going to slip into something more comfortable?"

"You wish."

"Indeed."

She laughed, delighted to see this side of him. "I'll take a club soda while you're at it."

"Glasses are in the kitchen?"

Sounded logical. She nodded, and then hurried down the small hall with the sudden hope that there were two bedrooms. Otherwise, she wasn't sure how she'd explain that.

The first door to the left was a bathroom, the yellow and orange living room colors repeated in its abstract wallpaper. Further down to the left was a nice-sized bedroom decorated in a surprisingly subtle palette of taupe and blue. Placed in the middle of the queen-sized bed was a piece of folded paper. Sara moved in closer to read the writing.

The sheets are clean, it read in large bold letters. Punctuated with a smiley face.

Sara quickly snatched the note and crumpled it in her hand. She turned around just as Cody appeared at the door. She jumped back, coming up against the bed and quickly having to steady herself. "Good grief, you scared me."

"Sorry, but you don't have any club soda." Scanning the room, his startled gaze briefly rested on the dresser, before he stared questioningly into her eyes.

She turned to see what had caught his attention. A picture of Chloe. Naked.

Sara sighed and with great reluctance, looked back at him. This was it. He was going to leave, and she'd never see him again. Wouldn't blame him one bit. He had to think she was a lesbian. Or at the very least, bi. "That's my roommate."

His eyebrows rose slightly. Clearly at a loss for words, he could only stare.

Sara decided that sticking as close to the truth as possible was her best avenue. "She's a nudist."

He frowned.

"She's also a practical joker."

His frown deepened. "Are you...?" He spread his hand as if he couldn't bear to finish the question.

She couldn't help but laugh. "No. Never. Not in this lifetime."

His mouth curved in a slight smile. "Good."

"Can't stand the thought of seeing me naked?"

Cody's eyes darkened. "Try me."

"Funny." She abruptly turned away to get rid of Chloe's picture. Damn, the man could reduce her to Jell-O with just a look. "I think I'd like something stronger than club soda, after all."

She approached him, and since he was blocking the door, she expected him to lead them out of the bedroom. Instead, he grasped her by the shoulders and kissed her lightly on the lips. She stiffened, even though she hadn't meant to.

He pulled back with a weary smile. "I'm hungry. How about you?"

"Starved."

He stepped aside to let her go first. As she left the room, she saw another door at the end of the hall to the right, which had to mean there was another bedroom. Unfortunately, he already thought this one was hers.

"So, I assume we're ordering dinner in," he asked,

once they'd returned to the living room. He went back to the small bar where he'd set out two glasses. Ironically, he already knew the apartment better than she did.

"I'm sure not cooking." She briefly studied the liquor offerings. "Is there any tonic?"

"Right here." He picked up the bottle. "Plain?"

"Add some gin."

He uncapped the bottle. "All right, back to dinner. Any preference?"

"I'm easy. You?"

His mouth started to slowly curve. "You'd be amazed how easy I am."

She flushed at his teasing, knowing if she lobbed the ball back into the same court, there would be no dinner. Nope, she wasn't ready quite yet.

"I'll check in the kitchen for takeout menus."

His shoulders sagged just enough to let her know he understood. Poor guy. She knew she was sending him mixed signals.

She headed for the kitchen, anxious to escape his probing eyes. "As I mentioned, I just moved in. And since it's a temporary arrangement…"

"Then what will you do?"

"Depends on what job I get." She found two menus held to the side of the refrigerator with magnets. "Chinese or Italian do anything for you?"

"Either one."

At the sound of his voice right behind her, she started. "Would you quit sneaking up on me?"

He handed her the gin and tonic. "I didn't think I had."

"No, of course not." She shook her head. "Sorry. It's been—"

"A bad day. I know." He took her free hand. "Come here."

She let him guide her to the living room, her heart beginning a slow steady beat. Then he took her drink and urged her to sit down. After placing both their glasses on the coffee table, he shrugged out of his suit jacket and sat beside her.

"Turn around," he said.

It took her a moment to realize what he wanted. The second she'd shifted and her back was to him, he pushed her hair aside and then started kneading the tension at the base of her neck. This man definitely had done this before. With his strong fingers, he followed the cords of muscle, applying the right amount of pressure to make her sigh with pure bliss.

"I assume I'm getting the correct spots," he said in a husky voice, his breath skimming her sensitized skin.

"Oh, baby."

He slid his hand down her upper arms, and she felt his lips on the side of her neck. She closed her eyes, allowing the pleasure of his touch to wash over her.

Right now, this second, with her eyes closed and the tension easing out of her shoulders, it all seemed like a dream. How many nights had she lain awake in her tiny Manhattan studio apartment, imagining that he was with her, both of them naked, him running his palms over her body?

Her fantasies had been so intense they'd actually

elicited dreams so vivid she had barely been able to meet his eyes the next day in the office. And now he was here. Touching her with his strong, capable hands, his warm breath on her neck and his hard body there for the taking. Making her wet and wanting. Maybe...

Oh, don't let it be a...

He dispelled any possibility that this wasn't real by crossing his arms over her breasts and pulling her back to lie against his chest. She clutched his forearm, and he apparently misunderstood because he loosened his hold and started to retreat.

Already having screwed up the kiss earlier, she quickly pulled his arms back around her, strategically placing one of his hands over her breast. His sharp exhale stirred her hair and she smiled. He hugged her closer and began to gently knead her breast.

"Sara?"

His gruff whisper took her breath away. She didn't speak, only tilted her head in answer.

"Look at me."

She turned around in his arms. His lips were parted, his lids lowered so that his eyes were only slits, but there was no mistaking the smoldering gleam that told her exactly what he wanted.

He lowered his head, and she lifted her mouth to his. Even though they'd already touched, when their lips met, everything changed. A fine tingling started at the crown of her head and traveled down her spine, straight to the dampness between her thighs.

It didn't help that he took his time, exploring the inside of her mouth with his tongue, leaving no inch untouched. This wasn't foreplay. It was sheer torture. Exquisite pain, but still.

Unable to stand it another moment, she broke the kiss long enough to turn around. Facing him took the torture to another level. She barely recognized the man. The feral color of his eyes darkened his face, and the normally stoic expression had morphed into pure desire.

He didn't seem in a hurry to resume the kiss. Instead, he touched her face. Gently, using the back of his hand, he stroked her cheek. And then he drew the tip of his finger across her damp lower lip before leaning in to reclaim her mouth.

She gladly submitted. The urge to touch him, and not only his face, was strong, but if she did, there would be no going back. This was it. The moment of decision. His low moan made it an easy one. As she pushed her tongue into his willing mouth, her hands moved to loosen his tie.

She felt the change in his kiss. They had crossed the border into uncharted territory. It took her a minute, but she finally got his tie undone. He, on the other hand, was far more dexterous and had her blouse all but unbuttoned. She yanked his shirt from his waistband. He did the same with her blouse.

Some part of her brain still persisted in worrying that they were going too fast. That they should talk more, get to know one another better. Then his knuckle lightly caressed her nipple.

"Oh, Sara," he whispered, pulling back to look at what he'd just touched.

She gave a silent thanks for push-up technology before she got busy taking off his shirt, only to be disappointed that he was an undershirt kind of guy. Not that she hated undershirts, but she really wanted skin. "Wouldn't you be more comfortable without that T-shirt?"

The corners of his mouth twitched as he reached for the hem. He pulled off the T-shirt, and she could only stare. She knew by feel that he was in great shape, but my, oh, my. This man definitely took good care of himself.

"Your turn." He didn't wait, but pushed the front of her blouse open. He ran his gaze from her breasts down to her belly. She'd barely had time to suck it in. "As pretty as that bra is," he said as he pushed the blouse off her shoulders, "I'd like it off."

The silk fabric slid down her back. "I'm sure you know how to handle that."

A slow sexy smile curved his mouth and within seconds he unfastened the front clasp and tossed her bra atop his jacket.

4

HER BREASTS were small and perfect all the way to the pink tips. He'd been hard for the last ten minutes; if he didn't unzip his fly soon, there'd be damage. And pain. When was the last time he'd wanted a woman like this?

It was definitely worth it. All of it. Coming to Atlanta for this menial case. Suffering Dakota and her annoying I-know-what-you're-up-to look. The curiosity from everyone in the office, including Teddy in the mailroom. Even enduring Gwen's undignified temper tantrum because he wouldn't be in New York to escort her to the Heart Ball that she was cochairing.

Cody knew he was insane, but right now he didn't give a damn. Sara was every bit as beautiful as he'd imagined.

"I didn't think you did anything but work." Sara flattened her palms against his chest and ran them up over his nipples, which promptly responded.

"Where did that come from?"

"You don't get a chest like this sitting at a desk."

He laughed, a little surprised at her bluntness. "I play tennis and jog. I even catch a pickup game of softball on the occasional Sunday."

"Are you serious?"

He touched the tip of one budded nipple, enjoying the way she shivered. Maybe now she'd stop talking and start doing far more interesting things.

She ran her hands back down his chest, to his belly, stopping right above his fly. "I can't imagine you playing softball."

"Why not?"

"Must be tough playing in a suit."

"Hey, I played baseball all through high school and for three years in college."

"Really?"

"Yes, really."

Instead of being satisfied and moving on, she looked even more curious. "Were you playing on a scholarship?"

"No." That would've pushed his parents over the edge.

"What happened the fourth year?"

"I decided to concentrate more on my studies."

"To get into law school."

He nodded. "You don't think it's rather absurd that we're both half-naked and talking about baseball?"

Sara smiled. "To be honest, this is killing me."

"I see," he said slowly as he palmed her right breast.

She moved into his touch, but just for a moment, and then settled back, her eyes full of misgiving. "Do you realize this is the most you've ever talked to me?"

"Not true."

"Okay, when have we had a decent conversation?"

"Back in New York." He tried not to stare at the

way her nipples had ripened. But then again, what the hell. She was the one making a game of this.

"When?"

"Many times."

"Give me a for instance." She folded her arms across her chest, cutting off his view.

"I spoke to you nearly every day."

Her eyebrows shot up. "Oh, right. Good morning, Sara. See you tomorrow, Sara. Is Dakota in her office? Have her call me when she gets in. Have you finished typing the Murphy briefs?" With a resigned shake of her head, she added, "I stand corrected. You talked to me all the time."

The earlier sarcasm had been much easier to take. She was being unreasonable. "The office is no place for small talk."

"You could've asked me to go for a drink after work. Oh, no, I forgot. I was just a peon."

"Well, honey, you could've asked me, too." He paused. "Or, wait, did *you* feel like too much of a peon?"

Anger sparked in her eyes. "Don't."

He looked away. Yes, she was right. But did she have to bring all this up now? His excitement from a minute ago had diminished, not because she wasn't still the most enticing woman he'd seen in years, but because she was clearly upset with him. That's not what he wanted for their first time. "Maybe we should order dinner."

She twisted around to get her blouse, letting him know unequivocally that he'd pegged the situation correctly. Dammit, she didn't understand. He was a senior partner with the firm, and senior partners simply did not ask temps out to dinner, or for drinks, or for anything else.

He got her bra and his shirt. After they'd both gotten dressed, he asked, "Do you want me to leave?"

She hesitated a moment too long.

Cody sighed as he got to his feet.

Sara touched his arm and stood, facing him, her blue eyes full of confusion. "Okay, I'm sorry. I don't know why I went off like that, especially when…" She winced, then gave him a sad smile. "Tell you what. Let's start over. Tomorrow."

"You sure?"

She nodded. "If you still want to."

He retrieved his jacket and shrugged into it. If he had an ounce of good sense, he'd leave things as they were. For a night that was supposed to have been about great sex and nothing but, things had gone from bad to worse. Did he want to risk this again? "Around six?"

"I think that'll be okay," she said, frowning and nibbling her lower lip. "I'll call."

"Look, if you don't—"

"No," she said quickly. "No, that's not it. I just can't remember if I have an appointment. I don't think so, but I want to be sure."

"You have my number?"

"It's in my cell."

She really was the most troublesome female. If only he hadn't thought about her so often. "I'll wait to hear from you."

She smiled and, to his astonishment, kissed him on the cheek. "I'll call you a cab."

"I'll do it when I get outside." He grabbed her around the waist and pulled her against him. Slipping his tongue between her surprised parted lips, he gave her a thorough kiss, touching the roof of her mouth and the fleshy insides of her cheek. He pulled back, satisfied with the dazed look on her face. "I'm going to need the fresh air," he said, and then left without looking back.

SARA GAVE UP trying to go back to sleep. Two more hours and she'd have to get up anyway. She had a meeting at nine and another one at two, and in between, lunch with an old family friend for whom she was considering working. After that, she was free for the day. That's when she planned on taking her small suitcase over to Chloe's apartment.

She turned on the bedside lamp and immediately caught sight of her cell phone sitting on the dresser, being charged. As soon as it was a reasonable hour, she'd call Cody. Not from her landline. No use letting him have the apartment number. She glanced around the large room, furnished with obscenely expensive pieces of art nouveau antiques. He could never come here. He wouldn't understand.

She'd already looked up a place for them to meet this evening. The Yellow Pages were full of bars and restaurants she'd never heard of, so she mostly chose by address. The farther on the other side of town, the better.

Yawning, she swung her feet to the carpeted floor and then stretched her arms above her head. Her stomach rumbled. No wonder, since she hadn't eaten anything since breakfast yesterday. Even worse, her coffeemaker wasn't programmed to start brewing for another two hours.

Sighing, she pushed herself toward the kitchen and manually started the coffee. Her stomach growled again and she checked the refrigerator, but there was only a quart of milk, a jar of strawberry jam and some low-fat margarine. She knew there was still some whole wheat bread in the pantry, which she found instantly since, sadly, that was the only thing on the shelves. Pretty bad when the pantry was the size of a small bathroom.

She popped two pieces of bread into the toaster, and then impatiently drummed her fingers on the mauve and gray granite countertop. Dammit. Why couldn't Shelby be here? As flaky as her sister could be, she was the one person Sara trusted implicitly. Even when Shelby was brutally honest, she was usually right. Probably because she didn't give a damn about politics or the opinions of their parents. She simply called it like she saw it.

An idea occurred to Sara just as her toast popped up. The next best thing to Shelby was the Eve's Apple Web site. She'd posted about Cody a few times when she was in New York, mostly because she'd been bored in the evenings and once because she'd had a particularly frustrating day with his royal highness.

Quickly she slathered her toast with margarine

and jam, and carried it sandwich-style on a paper towel, along with a mug of black coffee, back to her bedroom. Sitting on a gold-leafed table beside the burgundy chaise lounge was her laptop. She got comfortable on the chaise, stuck a piece of toast in her mouth and set the computer on her lap. It wasn't long before a bunch of crumbs ended up on her keyboard. Would she ever learn not to eat while she typed?

Muttering a mild curse, she took a bite and then set the rest of the toast on the paper towel. With a few taps on the keyboard, she found the saved Web site, and briefly scanned some of the recent posts. She hesitated, wondering how smart it was to have used her real first name and considered starting fresh. Although that was the only personal information she'd given about herself, other than mentioning that she was in Manhattan, but that was no big deal. Half the women who posted seemed to be from New York City.

Taking a deep breath, she started her post.

To: The Gang at Eve's Apple
From: Sara@EvesApple.com
Subject: His Royal Highness is back

No, he's not really royalty though he can be a royal pain in the ass. It's been a while since I posted but I really, really need to vent. I'd finally resigned myself to fantasies about HRH, and only fantasies, but what does he do? He shows up. Practically at my front door. Can anyone tell me what's up with that? I worked for his firm for months and he barely had anything to say to me.

Now, he's here. On my turf. (I should tell you that I moved back home so he actually had to travel to get here, albeit, he claims, on business.) The thing is, seeing him here isn't easy. Too many responsibilities and distractions. Don't recall if I told y'all that I'm recently out of school. New York was supposed to be my last fling, so to speak, before settling into reality.

<<Sigh>> The whole blessed thing is crazy. He's not my type, not that I know exactly what that is since I haven't dated a whole lot. In case you're wondering, studying took up a lot of time. Anyway, he's kind of a snob, definitely arrogant and basically has no use for someone like me in his life. So why, you ask, am I even interested? I haven't the faintest idea. Although he does have a great chest. And frankly, sex is all I'm after.

Sara abruptly stopped typing. "Oh, my God," she muttered, covering her mouth with one hand. Had she really just made that crude announcement? If her mother or grandmother, old-fashioned Southern ladies that they were, ever heard her...

But they wouldn't. That was the point of Eve's Apple. Anonymity. No holds barred. Even better than talking to Shelby, in some ways. Sara relaxed, and then continued with her post.

Okay, so I wouldn't be opposed to some feedback. I mean, I really am going for it. I think. But I wish this had all happened in New York.

Okay, hope all is well with all y'all. Wish me luck.
Tonight may be the night.
Hugs,
Sara

She reread what she'd written and then sent it off into cyberspace. Her gaze went back to the other posts and she felt badly for being so self-absorbed that she hadn't bothered to respond to any of the other women. She scanned a few and chose to respond to one that was pretty funny. At least the woman had a sense of humor about her man's eccentricities.

To: HornyInHouston@EvesApple.com
From: Sara@EvesApple.com
Subject: He's so fine
Dear Horny,
    I say, if he's willing to wear the French maid's uniform, too, then no harm, no foul. But if he expects you to be the only one playing dress-up, then I'd say bon voyage. But most importantly, does the relationship make you happy? Is it fun? Sounds like it from your post. Or do you feel like you have to play his game in order to keep him? I don't know. Just thinking out loud.
Hugs,
Sara

She signed off, closed her laptop and then stared off into space. Something about either the post or her reply made her feel heavyhearted. Horny had actually sounded quite humorous. And she seemed rather sure of herself, a little on the wild side, and not in any particular dilemma. But none of that stopped Sara from feeling unsettled. Was it possible she wanted something more than sex from Cody?

Nah.

Yet the chemistry was undeniable.

So why not go with it? No, it wasn't her typical style, and no, she didn't plan on making sex-only relationships the norm, but with Cody? As long as she was discrete and didn't end up in the gossip column of the newspaper. She reached for her cell and the paper with tonight's rendezvous address.

He should be up by now. And if not, she'd leave a message with the time and address of the bar. If he showed up, great. If not, she'd buy three pints of Häagen-Dazs ice cream to take with her to bed.

CODY'S GAZE drifted idly to the massive crystal chandelier that hung over the posh hotel lounge, finding it more and more difficult to concentrate on what Manning Junior was saying. Of course, none of his ramblings were germane to the case; he just liked hearing himself talk. At a thousand bucks an hour, Cody usually didn't mind, but he had to meet Sara in less than an hour.

"Hey, honey." His empty glass in his beefy hand, Junior waved for the leggy cocktail waitress in the short black tuxedo-like uniform, who promptly approached their table. "How about getting us boys a refill?" He put the glass on her tray, and winked at her abundant cleavage. "There's an extra fifty in it for you if you do it right quick."

The dark-haired young woman slid a glance at Cody. He gave a small shake of his head and mouthed that he wanted the check. She smiled and left, probably grateful she was off the hook. Manning was obviously really drunk. And Cody had been too damned preoccupied to notice.

Although, in his defense, it was as if a switch had been flipped. A few minutes ago, the guy had been totally coherent. Now his eyes were bloodshot and his speech slurred, his face flushed all the way to his receding blond hairline.

The waitress returned and before she could lay down the check, Cody immediately reached for it. He sure hoped Manning had a driver. Otherwise, it was going to be a bitch getting him to take a cab.

"What the hell are you doing?" Manning tried to grab the burgundy leather folder and nearly ended up facedown on the table.

Cody wanted to kick himself as much as he wanted to put a foot up the guy's ass. Dammit, he should've been paying attention. The last thing Junior needed was to be publicly intoxicated right before Cody negotiated a plea.

"We're leaving," he said in a low voice. People sitting at the next table had already shown interest. "Do you have your car, or did Sebastian drive you?"

"I'm not ready to go." Manning jerked upright and started looking around. "Where's that tall drink of water? You see the legs on that sweet young thing?"

"Harrison, keep your voice down." Cody pulled out cash. Forget the credit card. He needed to get Junior out of there now.

The younger man's bloodshot eyes narrowed. "Look, you work for me—"

"Not if you don't keep your damn mouth shut." Cody held his client's gaze until he looked away. At least he wasn't too drunk to understand the trouble he was in and how much he needed Cody's firm.

He slipped a large bill inside the leather folder holding the check. The exorbitant tip would be well worth it if he could get Manning out of the lounge right away and without attracting any more attention.

God, he hoped the guy could stand up by himself. Cody gave him the eye and then slowly got to his feet, watching Manning grip the arms of his club chair. He unsteadily pushed himself up, briefly losing his balance before righting himself. Fortunately, it seemed only the people at the table to the right noticed. Hopefully they were tourists.

Cody waited until Junior came up alongside him, and then they walked together toward the door, luckily without incident. Until they got outside.

"Is your driver waiting?" Cody asked, even though he saw no sign of the black limo and driver his client often used. He did, however, spot Manning's red Ferrari behind a midnight blue Mercedes convertible parked just off the porte cochere.

Damn.

A valet parker didn't even wait for Manning to say a word. Grinning, the young man trotted toward the car and climbed behind the wheel. Fortunately, the lineup of Jaguars and Mercedes would temporarily block the valet's progress and buy Cody some time.

He glanced at his watch and swore to himself. "Here's the deal, Harrison. Either you leave your car here and we call Sebastian, or I drive you home."

The shorter man's face, already flushed, got redder. "No one drives my car but me."

"Fine. We'll call Sebastian." Cody pulled out his cell phone.

"No, wait." Some of the belligerence was gone. He looked uncertain. "Shit." He shook his head and nearly lost his balance. "You drive," he said tersely, without looking at Cody. "Not a word of this to my father."

Cody nodded, and then they waited in silence for the car. He didn't bother looking at his watch again. If he was going to be late meeting Sara, he'd call her. He had no choice but to get Manning home safely. And tomorrow, when his client was sober, Cody was going to have one hell of a long talk with him. If Manning had a history of alcohol abuse, the case had just got a lot more complicated.

5

SARA DECIDED she was going to have to quit looking in the Yellow Pages for places to meet Cody. The place was huge, noisy, which wasn't helped by the seriously scuffed wooden floors and rowdiness over by the pool tables. The shells of the peanuts that the waitress automatically served with drinks apparently were meant to be tossed on the floor, because everyone was doing just that.

Only the large dance floor in front of the stage escaped the litter. She didn't know if that was the rule, or if the customers considered it some kind of sacrilege to mess up the area designated for two-stepping.

On the upside, she definitely wouldn't know anyone here at Billy Bob's. She took another sip of her club soda and repositioned her aching butt on the hard wooden bench.

She'd purposely chosen this booth so she could watch for Cody. Mostly so she could flag him down, but admittedly, it also was going to be fun seeing the look on his face when he first walked in.

Truthfully she herself hadn't really known what to

expect from a country and western bar, and she couldn't say she was totally comfortable. Five minutes after she'd arrived, some guy wearing too-tight jeans and with so much beer on his breath she'd nearly gagged had asked to buy her a drink. She'd been polite in her refusal, but his persistence had invited her temper. A few choice words and he'd disappeared.

She checked the time. Cody had called and said he might be about twenty minutes late. A half hour had already passed. She sighed and took another sip of her drink. At least this was an enriching cultural experience, what with the men in their cowboy hats and fancy buckles and western shirts. A few of the women wore Stetsons, too, and either skintight jeans or short denim skirts. Almost everyone wore pointy-toed boots.

"Hey, darlin', you shouldn't be sittin' here all by your lonesome." A husky man in his late twenties with vivid blue eyes slid into the booth opposite her. "How about I buy you another one of those that you're drinkin'."

"Thank you, but I'm waiting for someone."

He signaled the waitress. "You've been waiting a long time."

This wasn't personal, she reminded herself. He was just a guy in a bar, looking to pick up someone. "You've been watching me?"

"How could I drag my eyes away from a pretty little thing like you?"

The waitress appeared but before the jerk could say anything, Sara told her, "He's leaving."

Chuckling, the cowboy adjusted his hat and set it back on his head. He grinned at the uncertain waitress. "I'll take another—"

Sara leaned across the table and stared until she caught his gaze. "I mean it."

The waitress got the message and quickly moved to the next table.

The jerk's smile faded. "I like 'em feisty but that was plain rude."

"And sitting here uninvited isn't?"

"Fine," he said, sliding out of the booth. "Only tryin' to be friendly." With a cocky lift of his chin, he grabbed his beer off the table. "No need for you to go gettin' ugly about it."

She sighed as she watched him strut away. Did this represent the eligible guys out there? She hoped not. If so, it was no wonder there were so many women venting at the Eve's Apple Web site.

So far, all the country and western music, some of which she recognized, was coming from a juke-box. But a couple of guys had gotten up on the stage and seemed to be checking the sound equipment. She wondered when the band would start playing, and if that meant the dancing would also start. Great. All she needed was to be approached again. Cody had better hurry and get his attractive derriere here soon.

Her gaze went to the door and there he was. Still in his suit, D & G she guessed, looking as out of place as a hot fudge sundae in a frying pan. She at least was wearing jeans. She barely got her hand up to signal him when he saw her and started walking toward the table. He didn't look happy. He'd have to get over it.

"Sorry I'm late." He held his tie against his chest as he slid across the bench. "My meeting took longer than I'd anticipated."

"No problem." The way her heart sped up was horribly annoying. But he looked so darn good with his hair slightly disheveled and the stubble starting on his chin. "Everything going all right with your case?"

"Let's say I've had better days."

She tried not to smile. She knew the Mannings better than she'd let on. No doubt he'd have his hands full. "Well, now you can relax. Have some fun. I think the band is about to start warming up."

"Right." He eyed the pseudocowboy that stumbled past their table, leaving the stale odor of tobacco smoke in his wake.

"I know," she said, grinning. "I haven't been here, either, but—"

"So you choose this week to start branching out."

She laughed. "Come on. It's nice to step out of your comfort zone sometimes."

"You think I'm that broad-minded?"

"My point exactly."

His gaze met hers, and then rested on her white cotton shirt. Not exactly on her breasts but close enough to make her shift positions. "Oh, no. We're going to actually eat dinner tonight."

"I didn't say a word," he said, acting all offended. But his gaze moved up damn quickly.

The waitress came to take his drink order, which was a good thing because Sara truly did want to have a pleasant dinner before she took him home and rode him till they both cried mercy. She'd been wrong to push for the whole let's-get-to-know-each-other thing. She really needed to start thinking more like a guy. This wasn't about a budding relationship. This was about sex. That's all it could be about.

"So how did you find this place?" he asked as soon as the waitress left.

"Yellow Pages."

He smiled, and raised his brows expectantly.

"I really did."

"Seriously?"

She nodded.

"Why?"

She shrugged. "Something different. And I figured it would be noisy."

"You wanted that?"

"Let's just say it seemed a safer road."

"I suppose so," he said, not looking too thrilled. He scanned the room, his gaze lingering on the pool players. One of the guys bending over to take a shot wore jeans so low spectators could see far more than they wanted.

"Do you play pool?"

His gaze came back to her. But he said nothing, just stared, long enough for her to start feeling self-conscious.

She picked up her drink. "Okay, so you don't play pool."

"I used to play in college. We had a pool table at my fraternity house."

"Me, too. I played a little bit in college."

"Where did you go to school?"

She'd set herself up for that one. Stalling, she took a sip of her drink and then shrugged a shoulder. "You wouldn't know it. How good are you?"

"I'm very good."

"At pool."

"Ah." He smiled. "Fair."

She really liked his smile. Lines radiated from his eyes going all the way to his temples and down toward his ears. He'd probably hate it if she pointed that out. But it didn't make him look old, just a bit weathered, an amazingly attractive contradiction to his impeccable image.

"How old are you?" she asked suddenly.

He frowned. "Thirty-five. Why?"

"Just wondering."

The waitress came with his drink and left them two menus. Sara quickly grabbed hers.

He ignored his. "Something prompted your curiosity."

With great reluctance, she dragged her fascinated gaze away from the large selection of chili dogs. They sure as hell didn't serve those at La Maisonette. "I was just wondering why you've never married."

"What makes you think I haven't?" He nonchalantly picked up his menu.

She gaped. "You have?"

"No." His lips curved in a small smile as he pretended to be interested in the menu.

"You're a rat."

"How original." He frowned at the menu. "Is grease included in every item?"

"We're going for the unfamiliar, remember?"

"You've done a great job."

She grinned. "I'm having the nachos with everything. Ooh, and onion rings."

"Seriously?"

She nodded enthusiastically. Most of the time, she watched what she ate, confining herself to more salads than a person should have, but this was a night for indulgence. In all kinds of ways. She closed the menu and smiled at Cody.

"Hmm," he said, as his gaze went back to his food choices.

"What does that mean?"

"Weren't you the woman who brought a salad to work every day, in the same brown paper bag?"

"Well, actually, I brought the salad in a plastic bowl, and I put that into the bag."

His right eyebrow shot up.

"Okay, so— Hey, how did you know?"

He quickly went back to the menu. "My secretary must have mentioned it."

"Is that so?"

He ignored her as he turned the page.

She had to admit it tickled her to pieces that he'd noticed a detail like that. She supposed she could cut him a break. "What are you having?"

Lacking enthusiasm, he looked up. "Are you sure you don't—"

"I'm positive."

Amusement gleamed in his eyes. "You know what I was going to say?"

"You want to go someplace else."

"Filet mignon and a lobster tail with drawn butter. Maybe tiramisu for dessert. Sound good?"

She leaned toward him. "You do understand this is only about sex," she whispered and was rewarded with a look of absolute shock. "You don't have to wine and dine me."

He opened his mouth, but nothing came out. He just shook his head, looking totally bewildered.

Sara laughed, not feeling quite as brazen as she sounded. "Come on. Admit it. That's really why you got on that plane in New York."

"You're crazy."

"You don't know the half of it." Her cell phone rang, startling her, because she didn't think she had it turned on. She thought about ignoring it, but couldn't resist and checked the caller ID.

Damn.

"Would you excuse me?" she said, and with phone in hand, quickly slid out of the booth.

IT WASN'T in Cody's nature to be curious, but she had him in a tailspin. He hadn't met anyone like her. The women he dated were all pretty much the same. Upper-class society types who dressed well, spoke carefully and made careers of spending money.

When he took them out, they expected only the finest restaurants, the best theatre seats. Sara wanted nachos and onion rings?

He watched her, the phone to her ear, hurrying toward the front door. It wasn't that noisy that she couldn't have heard the caller, which meant she obviously didn't want him to hear the conversation. Which was okay. She was certainly entitled to her privacy, but her apparent secretiveness since he'd arrived did make him wonder.

The band started playing a country and western song, and he sighed. Faint background music was all right but this was ridiculous. Even the waitresses' uniforms were on the absurd side. Short denim skirts and white cowboy boots. The damn peanut shells were everywhere, including stuck to the bottom of his Italian loafers. He sure hoped that she didn't plan on staying here long.

Although, they could always play pool. Right. His gaze went to the tables. Actually, that wasn't a bad idea. He wasn't great but back in the day he'd beaten three out of five guys pretty regularly. He'd make a wager with her. If he won, he'd get to choose where they'd go tomorrow night.

When he looked over his shoulder toward the door, she was already headed back to the table. Her snug jeans showed off nicely rounded hips and long slender legs. A couple of guys sitting at the bar turned around to watch her walk past them and an unfamiliar wave of jealousy swept over him.

"Sorry about that," she said as she slid into the booth.

"Everything all right?"

She nodded. "The band's loud."

"Too loud. We can still leave."

Sara grinned. "How about I sit next to you so we don't have to shout at each other?"

"Excellent idea." Not that he was surprised but at the mere suggestion, his cock twitched.

She got up and came around the table. He moved over, but not much. Her thigh pressed against his and a whiff of her soft perfume made him slightly heady. She knew how to wear the right amount—intoxicating without being cloying.

"Are you ready to order dinner?" she asked, her breath brushing his ear.

He didn't answer, but hooked a finger under her chin as he kissed her. Lightly, a mere touching of lips, until hers parted. He accepted the invitation and pushed the tip of his tongue inside. Not even acknowledgment of this insanity stopped him. He despised vulgar public displays yet here he was, unable to pull away or keep his cock from getting harder than the bench he sat on.

Sara retreated first, the shock on her face reflecting his own. Discreetly, she glanced around and then looked at him again. "At least we don't know anyone here," she said with a nervous laugh.

"Right." He straightened. Last time he'd been this indiscreet was in eighth grade when his mother caught him making out with Lindsey Hastings in the backyard pool. Well, except for the fraternity years, but those didn't count.

"I'm not complaining, mind you." She laid a hand

on his thigh, and he hoped like hell she didn't go too far up because she might find more than she bargained for. "But I think a little more privacy is in order."

"Agreed," he said, tensing when her hand moved up. "Ah, I thought you said—" He shifted when she reached the danger zone. "Careful."

She laughed softly. "No one can see under the table."

"That's true." He slipped a hand between her thighs, and she jumped. "What's the matter?"

She bumped him with her shoulder. "You're evil." And then she withdrew her hand and picked up the menu. "I think it's time we ordered."

Reluctantly, he, too, withdrew. "Right, and then after we eat, let's play a game of pool."

She turned to look at him. "Really?"

"Sure."

"All right," she said with a slight frown. "But I'm pretty rusty."

"Me, too. Since it would seem we're equally matched, let's make it interesting."

Her gaze narrowed in suspicion. "How?"

"Just a small wager."

"And that would be?"

"Hmm." He pretended to think for a moment. "Whoever wins chooses where we go tomorrow night."

Her expression fell. "I don't think I'm free to-morrow."

God, he wanted to kick himself. What an ass he was. "Right. Didn't mean to be presumptuous."

"No, I'm flattered. But I have this dinner that I have to attend."

"I understand."

The waitress showed up to take their food order, saving him from digging a deeper hole. Sara already knew what she wanted, and he figured a cheeseburger would be okay. It even sounded good. He was careful about what he ate, and it had been a while since he had anything like a burger and fries.

The band started another number, a popular dance song judging from the whoops and hollers and the rush to the dance floor. This was certainly a different world. As much as he enjoyed the feel of Sara pressed against him, he wanted to see her face, to study her reaction to the couples dancing, to the slob at the bar who hadn't stopped eyeing her.

Was this close to her world? She might really have used the Yellow Pages to find a place new to her, but the fact that she was so reticent to go to a restaurant of his choosing made him wonder if she was uncomfortable with fine dining.

For a place this size, the food got to the table awfully fast. Sara moved back to the other side of the table because there wasn't enough room for everything she ordered on one side. She wasn't shy about digging in. She attacked the nachos and onion rings with an enthusiasm that made him both smile and wince. Amazingly, she got nothing on the tailored white cotton shirt she wore.

By the time he finished his burger, she was only halfway through her meal, but she laid down her napkin, and said, "Ready for a game of pool?"

He looked over at the tables, two of which were

available. The thing was, since he couldn't see her tomorrow night, he didn't particularly want to waste the time they had playing pool.

"What's the matter? Afraid I'm going to humiliate you?" she asked sweetly.

"Right."

She laughed. "Now is probably a good time before the band takes a break."

"I was actually thinking we should go to a place that's more quiet."

"Come on. One game." She was already sliding out of the booth.

Cody sighed. At least it shouldn't take long. Reluctantly he got to his feet.

"Look, we can still make a bet if that would make you feel better."

He smiled grudgingly. "What's the prize?"

"Winner's choice?"

"You're on." He pulled off his tie and then took off his jacket. "You go grab a table and I'll get the check."

"But—"

"After I beat you, we're leaving."

Laughing, she grabbed her drink. "We'll see," she said over her shoulder, and then headed for one of the empty tables.

Their waitress happened by and she stopped and leafed through a stack of checks on her tray. She found theirs and he took care of it, leaving yet another huge tip in his haste.

Sara was already checking out the cues when he joined her. She seemed much pickier, choosing a cue and rolling it on the table to make sure it wasn't curved, then putting it back and selecting another. Maybe he should rethink this winner's choice deal.

Finally, she found one to her liking and looked up at him. "Do you want to rack them or shall I?"

"Are you hustling me?"

"Me?" She winked. "Not a chance."

"Now why do I find that hard to believe?" he asked, as he put his quarters into the table and waited for the balls to fall. She stood close, chalking her cue in a way that made his mouth water.

God, he had it bad if even the cues made him jealous.

Racking quickly, he let her break. His heart sank the moment the white ball struck. She'd pocketed no less than three balls, two solid and one stripe.

He moved to the far wall in order to watch her in motion. Man, she was something in those jeans. There were so many women he knew who starved themselves into unattractiveness, their bones sticking out and absolutely nothing to grab on to. Not Sara, which he appreciated very much. So much, in fact, that he wanted this silly game over and done with so he could see her without the jeans.

Just to make things more painful, Sara moved in front of him to make her next shot. She had to bend over, of course, but he didn't think she had to do it quite so slowly, or bend quite that much.

She was a tease, all right. A tease who shot damn good pool.

"Hmm," she said, chalking up once more. "That leaves the two, the six and the ten for me. And what is it for you?" She counted each of his remaining stripes, one after the other, in a voice so sweet he could add it to his coffee.

"You vixen," he said.

She laughed out loud. "Vixen? Have you been reading those Southern Gothic romances, you Yankee devil?"

Some guy moved in front of him, and put a couple of quarters on the table. It didn't matter, because they were leaving after this game, but damn, did he have to stand right there?

"Hey, darlin'. Wipe this guy's balls up with that pretty cue o' yours and let's have a real game."

Cody moved closer to the table in time to see Sara twirl on the cowpoke like a fury.

"Excuse me, I'm in the middle of a conversation."

The faux cowboy turned in his two-bit boots to stare at Cody. "That loser?" His voice slurred on the word. "Honey, you're in a country bar now. You don't have to settle for that other white meat no more. Not when there's prime beef on the counter."

"Hey, beef," Cody said, his temper shooting from zero to ninety in two seconds.

"I've got it," Sara said, closing in on the interloper. "I told you before. You're not welcome here. I'm with the gentleman."

The drunkard pointed a quavering finger at Cody. "A fine-looking woman like you can do so much better."

That was it. Cody didn't know if they had bouncers in this yahoo place before, but they had one now. No way anyone was going to talk to his woman like that.

He put the cue down. "Step away from the table, buddy," he said. "You're leaving, and I mean right this minute."

"Cody, I've got it," Sara said. She put her cue on the table and turned on the cowboy. "Get the hell out before you get hurt."

He laughed, but it was the last sound he was gonna make with an unbroken jaw, if he kept it up. He tapped the idiot on the back, and as the man turned, Cody pulled his arm back.

He hadn't seen Sara come around and make her move until the drunk ducked and then her elbow smashed into Cody's eye. Pain exploded in his face and he reeled back, bumping into the bar stool.

She gasped. The drunk laughed. Cody swore as he regained his balance. Now, he was really pissed.

6

"OH, NO!"

Sara put a hand on Cody's arm, but he shook her away. The rage in his face made her shudder. His hand fisted. She couldn't believe she'd hit him instead of the drunk, but if she didn't do something now, the whole situation would get a lot worse.

She stepped between Cody and the other man. "Leave. Now."

The guy opened his mouth, but before a word came out, Sara shoved him back. "Listen, you pathetic drunk. I can hurt you in ways you never even dreamed of."

The man wiped his sloppy mouth with the back of his arm. "You're a feisty little thing. I like 'em that way," he said, and then reached for her.

She caught his wrist and pulled his arm up against his back until he groaned and cut loose with a pithy four-letter word. "Not only will I hurt you," she whispered. "But I'll also embarrass the hell out of you. Or you can walk away. Make up your mind."

"Bitch," he ground out.

She yanked his arm up harder. The guys playing

at the next pool table had stopped to watch and started laughing.

"Let me go." He struggled, but she knew how to keep him immobile.

"Are you going to behave?"

"Yeah, yeah."

She immediately released him. But only because Cody had stepped around her to take over the brawl. The drunk looked up at Cody's face, and all his bravado fizzled. For a moment, Sara was insulted. She'd had the bastard in one hell of an armlock. Another inch, and she'd snap him like a twig. But was he afraid of her?

Then she caught sight of Cody's reddened eye, and her ego deflated. She stepped out of the way of the drunk, who was squealing like a piglet. He ran between the pool tables, skirting the ire of Cody.

Cursing herself for a fool, she hooked an arm around Cody's. "Let's go," she said.

He started to resist, and then grabbed his jacket off the bar stool and allowed her to lead him outside. They both kept their faces straight ahead, and she wished she'd brought her car.

As soon as they were outside, he asked, "Where did you learn that move?"

At the resentment in his voice, she looked sharply at him. "I'm sorry, okay, but it was an accident."

"I'm not talking about hitting me. I meant the armlock."

"Oh. I had some self-defense classes."

"I'll bet."

"Really, I am sorry." She turned to look at his eye and winced at the bruise that had already started showing. Shaking her head, she hit the speed dial number for the local cab company. Someone answered on the other end, and she gave them the address.

"I'm sorry, too. You shouldn't have had to deal with an ass like him. Where are we going, anyway?"

"To my place. I'll get you cleaned up."

He gingerly touched the area around his eye. "This is great. Just great."

"I'm sorry."

"You don't have to apologize. You were protecting yourself. My face just got in the way."

She pretended to look for the cab, although it was obviously too soon. She knew Cody was right— she'd done nothing to provoke the baboon who'd started the fight—but she felt horrible, because she'd brought him to this place. She had taken the easy way out, and it had gotten him hurt. She should have been honest with him from the moment he'd come to Atlanta. She'd screwed things up, big-time, and there was no one to blame but herself.

"Hey." He caught her by the chin and forced her to look at him. "None of what happened was your fault and it wasn't mine. The guy was an idiot. Case closed."

Sara smiled. "Spoken like a true lawyer."

His face darkened, and he moved his hand to his eye. "What?"

"This is going to look terrific if I have to show up in court day after tomorrow."

"I thought the case would be handled out of court."

He sighed wearily. "I'm not sure."

"Something happen?" She thought she saw a cab stopped at the intersection and stepped out into the street for a better look, prepared to flag it down.

"Look out!" Cody grabbed her arm and jerked her back onto the sidewalk.

A dirty black pickup truck missed hitting her by a foot. The guy sitting in the passenger seat stuck his head out the window and yelled something foul. Of course, it was the drunk.

"Stupid bastard." Cody's focus stayed on the truck as he pulled a BlackBerry out of his jacket pocket. He started to record the license number, but Sara stopped him.

"Don't," she said. "Just let it go."

He looked at her in disbelief and then finished writing the plate number. "That guy could have killed you."

"I'm not pursuing this." Publicity was the last thing she needed. Her family, all of Atlanta, would know she'd been slumming.

The unbidden, unkind thought stopped her cold. How could she? She wasn't that kind of person. She wasn't a snob. Bad enough her knees were still shaking from the near miss; the self-disgust she felt made her sick to her stomach. "Look, there's our taxi. Please, can we just leave?"

The stubborn set of his jaw didn't bode well, but then he nodded. The cab pulled up to the curb, and he opened the door for her. She hesitated before getting in, ready to tell him everything. But once he was beside her and he touched his swelling face, she lost her nerve.

CODY SETTLED onto the couch in Sara's living room and, wincing, probed the area around his eye. He didn't want to look in the mirror. The skin had to be discolored already. He would look like a wreck tomorrow. And the next day.

He still wanted to call the police and have the guy picked up. Sara could've been killed, but for whatever reason, she adamantly wanted to ignore the incident. The next time they went out, assuming there'd be a next time, he was calling the shots. No more stepping outside their comfort zones. He gingerly felt his nose. It hurt like hell, but at least it wasn't broken.

"All right. Let's see if this helps." Sara sat beside him, holding a bag of frozen peas and a paper towel.

"What is that for?"

"We need to try and keep the swelling down." She wrapped the paper towel around the bag and pressed it to his injured eye.

"This is your version of an ice pack?"

"It works. Trust me. I had a big knot on my forehead once and this is exactly what I used."

He settled back so that he could keep the bag of peas in place and still be able to look at her. "How did you get the knot?"

"Playing lacrosse. Oh, no, you got something icky on your shirt." She studied the spot. "It's not much, but I should soak it in some water."

He moved the peas from his face. "You play lacrosse?"

"I used to."

"When?"

"Come on, take the shirt off."

He started unbuttoning, silently lamenting how the evening was supposed to have gone. Then she started helping, her deft fingers brushing his skin as she undid each button, and he thought maybe all was not lost.

"Come on, tell me when you played lacrosse."

She pulled back, looking uncertain, looking as if she wanted to change the subject. He thought back to the cab ride. He'd been certain she'd wanted to tell him something, but when he'd asked, she'd changed the subject to the one thing that was sure to distract him. They'd ended up talking about the Braves and the Mets. Smart girl. It was possible she was truly interested in the team, but he would lay odds that she had used a classic redirect. He thought about coming right out and asking her if she had something to say, but the truth was, he wasn't sure he wanted to know.

Still, the lacrosse remark made him wonder. Most likely she'd played while she was a student. But only exclusive private schools offered that type of activity.

"Where did you say you played?" he asked again.

She moistened her lips. "In high school."

"Oh?"

"Did you play?"

"Don't change the subject."

She briefly looked away. "I went to Andover."

He stared at her, wondering if she was joking. "Andover?"

"My grandfather insisted."

"Don't sound apologetic. Andover is one of the

best prep schools in the country." Tuition, he knew, was astronomical. Her parents had to have some serious dough to afford to send her there. Or maybe her grandparents had the money. That might account for her expensive accessories on a temp's salary.

"I know." She readjusted the bag of peas he'd let slide. "I'm very thankful for such a good education."

"What college did you say you went to?"

"I didn't." She scooted closer to him. "How much do you hurt?"

"Depends."

"On?" She slid a palm up his thigh.

"I don't feel a thing." He put the pseudo ice pack on the console table behind the sofa and reached for her.

"No." She snatched it back and held it to his eye. "Seriously, you need to reduce the swelling."

"But I thought—"

She put a finger to his lips. "Don't think. Don't move. Just lie back."

Cody exhaled slowly. She was a sly one. How could he think about anything else when she kept stroking higher up his thigh? Why would he want to? He sucked in a breath when she grazed his fly, already bulging from his hardening cock. He groaned.

She stiffened and her hand slipped away. "Was that an ouch or a pleasure groan?"

He didn't say anything, just put her hand back on his fly.

"Oh, good." She smiled and started on his belt buckle, quickly disengaging it. After she undid the snap, she took the zipper halfway down and then stopped. "I would've bet a month's salary you were a briefs kind of guy."

He smiled. "There's a lot you don't know about me."

"Ditto."

Now was the perfect time to ask what she'd meant earlier, but he didn't care. "Take your blouse off."

She shook her head. "I'm calling the shots."

Her nipples were hard and protruding beneath her white shirt. He took one between his thumb and forefinger and lightly pinched. She gasped and, briefly closing her eyes, pushed against his hand.

"Your blouse," he said, almost pleading.

She went back to unzipping his fly.

He cursed under his breath and got rid of the ridiculous bag of peas. She started to protest but he caught her by the wrist and pulled her up with him as he got to his feet, which proved tricky until he got his trousers fastened.

"What are you doing?" she asked, wide-eyed and breathless, but not resisting.

"I don't want a replay of last night. We're going to your bedroom."

"But your eye—"

"Sara."

Her face softened. "All right."

He let her go ahead of him, and he followed her to her room. It looked different from last night, but then he hadn't paid much attention. She switched on one of the lamps, and while he took off his unbuttoned shirt and kicked off his shoes, she pulled back the black-and-white comforter. The sheets were the same abstract design, which somehow didn't suit her.

She turned to him, her gaze going to his chest and lingering there. "I really should soak that shirt."

"If I don't have anything dry to wear, I'll have to spend the night."

She gave him a sexy smile and started unbuttoning her blouse. "Is that a problem?"

"None whatsoever."

"Perfect."

"Ditto."

Laughing, she undid her last button and then freed the cuffs.

His impatience at getting her naked surprised him. Of course he'd always enjoyed sex and he was lucky enough to have had a variety of eager partners, but something about Sara taunted him even when he wasn't with her. He hoped like hell that coming to Atlanta and seeing her a final time—even better, bedding her—would rid him of his obsessive thoughts.

"Need help?" he finally asked when she seemed to be taking her sweet time.

"Impatient?"

"Very."

Her lips curved in a wicked smile, and with painstaking slowness, she undid the front closure of her bra. "Why are your pants still on?"

"Impatient?"

Her smile widened. "Very."

"Good." He caught her arm and pulled her toward him. Quickly, he got rid of the bra and then unfastened her jeans. She helped by unzipping them and then wiggling her hips as he pulled the jeans down near her ankles. She kicked off her sexy high-heeled sandals and then rid herself of the jeans. All that was left was a triangle of black silk at the juncture of her thighs and silky skin.

He stepped back to look at her, and she visibly shivered, bringing her arms close to her body and looking as if she wanted to hide. The idea was absurd. She was incredible. Perfect in every way.

"Come here," he said hoarsely. "If I keep looking at you, I won't be responsible for my actions."

She smiled shyly and stepped into his arms. The feel of her soft bare breasts against his chest made his groin ache. But he didn't want to rush if he could help it. He really wanted to take his time, explore every part of her, learn her likes and dislikes. But it wasn't going to be easy pacing himself.

He ran his palms down the curve of her back until he reached the top of her skimpy panties. He toyed with the elastic for a moment and then slid his hands beneath, molding his palms over her firm derriere. She pushed against him, her nipples hard and teasing.

"You're overdressed," she whispered, her warm breath caressing his throat. And then she unsnapped his trousers and, with little effort, slid them down to where he could step out of them.

Normally he'd hate leaving his suit pants in a pool

on the floor, but right now they were the last thing he cared about. He cupped her generous bottom, reveling in the feel of her pressed against his rock-hard cock. She tipped her head back and he claimed her mouth with a savagery that was foreign to him. Maybe back in high school or college he'd felt this primal urge to possess a woman like this, but it had been so long he couldn't remember.

She kissed him back with equal urgency and fiercely tugged at the waistband of his boxers. Apparently unsatisfied with her progress, she slipped her hand inside and took hold of him. Gently exploring the head and then stroking down to the base. He shook with need but he had to stop her. They had to take their time. She got to the smooth tip and ran a finger around just the right spot.

Screw it. They didn't have to take their time. They had all night.

SARA WAS SO WET she had to squeeze her thighs together when he suddenly scooped her up and held her against his chest. Not that she knew what clamping her legs shut accomplished. It was purely reflexive. Or maybe because she was a bit self-conscious. But when Cody laid her down on the bed and stared at her as if she were the most beautiful woman in Atlanta, all other fears and insecurities fled.

He sat beside her and touched the tip of one nipple, his gaze fixed on it as if he were totally mesmerized, as if he'd never seen one before. Then he lowered his head and took a taste. She closed her eyes and drew in her lower lip as he pulled off her panties. He switched to the other nipple and laid a hand on her belly, the tips of his fingers skimming the nest of hair.

With effort, she opened her eyes but her vision blurred. She blindly reached for his boxers, and he helped her get them off. She moved closer to the center of the bed and he stretched out beside her. She was so aroused she had to touch him, feel the hard length of him. But when she tried, he moved out of her grasp.

"Hey. Not fair." She lightly punched his arm.

"And your point is?"

"I'll show you—"

He cupped one of her breasts and greedily suckled it. She squirmed, trying to get away, but the move gave him entrance and he slipped his hand between her thighs. He slipped two fingers inside her and her resistance vanished in a pool of desire.

He'd been right to bring them to the bedroom. This had been the goal, the reason she'd done it all. To be with Cody was to have her fantasies come to life, and she wasn't going to let anything, especially a guilty conscience, spoil things.

She put her hand on the back of his head, plunging her fingers into his thick hair, letting him know she appreciated his talented tongue, not to mention the little nips with his teeth. She'd forgotten just how sensitive her nipples were.

Her moan, however, wasn't from the attention to her breast. He had found her clit with the soft pad of his thumb, and as he pumped into her slowly with his fingers, he used that thumb in wicked small circles.

She had to move, to spread her legs more, to give him all the access he needed. Once she'd settled, he moved his mouth to her other breast, never missing a stroke down below.

Bending her head, she kissed the top of his head, then ran her hand down his back. She couldn't reach too far, but he didn't seem to mind. His muscles rippled as she touched him and his pace quickened.

"Sensitive, hmm?" she asked, already knowing the answer.

He moaned in response. She used her fingernails across his shoulders, and he shivered for her. It made her smile that he was so responsive. Imagine what he'd do when she touched his cock.

Now that she'd thought of it, she had to see. Yes, it meant making him stop what he was doing, but she had all the faith in the world that he'd find something else equally pleasurable.

She pulled away from him, delighting in his wounded expression. Keeping her eyes on his face, she moved her hand from his back to his hip, then slid around until her fingers just touched his thick erection.

He didn't moan this time. He hissed as if she'd burned him, but there was pleasure in his pain. It was all there on his handsome face. Tense muscles, flared nostrils, his eyes darkened and full of fire.

"You're playing a dangerous game," he said, his voice barely more than a growl.

"I can take care of myself," she said.

"Not like I can," he said. An instant later, he was on his knees, gripping her shoulders. He pulled her up, only to put her down again on her back, her head on the pillow. He moved his knees between her thighs and eased her legs further apart. Then he reached over to the nightstand. She didn't have to look to know he was getting the condom out of his wallet. Her focus was entirely on what would happen after the condom was on.

She closed her eyes, aching to touch him, to feel every part of him.

How many nights had she dreamed of this? Pictured him above her, his eyes wild, all his reserve stripped, leaving him naked—not just physically, but emotionally.

When his hands slid under her knees and he lifted her legs to his shoulders, she knew she'd gotten even more than she'd hoped for.

Her eyes opened as he bent forward. He stared right at her as he moved into position. She felt his blunt cock head at her entrance and then, as he leaned even further, he started to push.

Slowly, slowly, he filled her. It had been so long, so lonely and so worth the wait. Tremors shook her body as the connection between them tightened. He wasn't just with her, he was part of her.

No, she couldn't take care of herself like this. Her fantasies had been laughable now that she had the real thing to compare them to. The least of it was the sex itself. It was the intimacy. The way he let down his guard. The desire that was so clear in his eyes.

"Sara," he whispered.

Her mouth opened, but she couldn't speak. He was in her completely now and it was the most incredible sensation.

"Come with me, Sara," he said as he began to move.

It was only later, after she'd almost passed out from the most amazing climax she'd ever had, that she wondered if his invitation had been about her orgasm or much, much more.

7

DAKOTA PUT her briefcase and purse by her apartment door, checked her watch and, deciding she had a few minutes to spare, went to her computer in the small den that was no more than a closet.

It had been months since she had been to the Eve's Apple Web site. Even before she and Tony had gotten together, she'd stopped posting. Although one of the draws to the site was anonymity, Dakota had read a post that she suspected had been authored by Sara. The idea that someone Dakota knew could be reading her lunatic rants had soured her on posting. However, she had been careful about not revealing too much information.

Sara, on the other hand, had used her real name, identified Manhattan as the city where she lived and talked about the arrogant snob where she worked that had to be Cody. Dakota loved her brother, but he definitely had issues regarding where he should fit on the social scale. She didn't fault him entirely. Their parents had played a major role in molding Cody at an early age.

If they'd had their way, all three of their children

would have become lawyers. She and Cody had succumbed, but not Dallas. Maybe because he was the oldest and hit the hardest, Cody had dutifully followed the path they'd laid out for him. Going to the right schools, the right dinner parties, dating women who, if one of them eventually became his wife, would advance his career. Brilliant and enviable as his career was, he'd missed out on so much. He didn't see it. She did. So did Dallas, but they were his younger sisters and their opinion couldn't convince him.

Tough. If she was right about Sara being the one who'd posted, then this was Dakota's chance to pull a few strings, and she'd be damned if she wouldn't. There wasn't a single reason that Cody had to handle that case in Atlanta. Not a professional reason, anyway.

She quickly scanned the site, looking for posts that were dated right before Cody left. She had no way of knowing if he'd contacted Sara before leaving, but if she knew her brother, he'd have waited until the last minute. Sure enough, she found Sara's post the day after Cody had arrived.

Dakota read it and smiled. Of course she wouldn't say anything to Cody, but good for him for taking the step. Sara would be great for him. She was smart and genuine. The women he usually dated might help advance his career, but they were the type who only dated him because of how much he had to offer financially and socially.

She sank back in her chair, trying to decide what

action she should take, if any. As much as she hated to interfere, she didn't want Cody blowing this opportunity. Maybe if she just called him…

"Hey, honey."

At the sound of Tony's voice behind her, she logged off, and then turned around and smiled. "What are you doing awake?"

He yawned and rubbed his unshaven chin. "It's almost seven-thirty. I thought you were going in early." His curious gaze went to the computer screen. But there was nothing there for him to see.

She got to her feet. "I'm on my way out." She stopped to kiss him, but knew better than to linger. He'd end up talking her back into bed. And to think she'd almost blown her chance with him. All because others thought he wasn't right for her. She'd been lucky because Tony hadn't given up on her. It was time for her to give back. And not let Cody screw up his life.

"ARE WE done here?" Manning pushed the plea agreement across the table. He'd barely looked at it. "I could use a drink."

The was the last thing he needed. Cody's patience was running out. "Did you read it?"

"I'm not pleading to anything. Your job is to make this thing go away."

"Hell, Manning, you broke the guy's nose. You're getting off easy."

"Bullshit." The younger man's face reddened. "I didn't do anything. He just wants the money."

Cody frowned. "What about our initial conversation?"

"What about it?" Fear flickered in the man's eyes, quickly replaced with belligerence.

Cody closed his eyes and pinched the bridge of his nose. This was not good. The guy didn't remember his admission. Had he been drinking the first time Cody had spoken with him? This supposedly nothing case was turning out to be a big mess.

"So, are you going to fix this?"

Staring him straight in the eyes, Cody waited until he had his client's full attention. "Have you been drinking today?"

"No."

"Nothing?"

"Not since lunch."

Sighing, Cody threw down his pen.

"What the hell difference does it make if I had one stinking scotch?"

"If the jury thinks you're a drunk, who do you think they're going to believe? You or the gardener?"

Manning yanked his tie loose. Sweat beaded above his upper lip. "This can't go to trial."

"It will if you don't accept this plea agreement."

"I thought you were the best." The belligerence was back in his voice and in the set of his jaw.

Cody summoned all the control he could marshal, when what he really wanted to tell him was that no one could help a loser. "It is my opinion that you should take this offer."

"Hell, no."

"A trial will bring a lot of negative publicity."

"I'm not doing any goddamn community service. It's not gonna happen."

"All right, then we are done." Cody gathered up the papers and deposited them into his briefcase.

"Wait a minute," Manning said when Cody stood. "What happens now?"

"Your father can find you another lawyer."

"You can't tell my father about me turning down the plea agreement. This is privileged information." He looked nervous, as well he should. "Right?"

"Right."

The corners of his mouth turned up in a smug smile. "So?"

"I'm not telling your father a thing." Cody swung his briefcase off the table. "But I'm sure he'll have a few questions for you when I tell him I'm withdrawing as your counsel."

"Jesus Christ, Shea. Can't we work this out?"

"Apparently not." Cody left the conference room, hoping like hell his bluff would work. The senior Manning was too important a client to piss off, and Cody didn't know what his reaction would be if Cody really quit.

The office in the Manning building where they'd met was just three blocks from his hotel, definitely walking distance. He was going to get to see Sara after all, but since she wouldn't be free until nine tonight he was on his own for dinner. First, he had to dump his briefcase, then change his clothes. Although he hadn't brought anything casual to wear, only suits. And God only knew where Sara would ask him to meet her tonight.

His hand automatically went to the corner of his right eye. This morning he'd looked into the mirror first thing. The discoloration turned out to be as bad as he'd expected. There was nothing to do about it except stick to his story that he'd run into a valet cart coming off the hotel elevator and hit his eye on the clothes bar.

As foolish as he felt, especially with the strange looks he'd gotten, he'd do it all over again if it meant ending up in Sara's bed. Trying not to think about what they'd done in her bed had been a struggle all day. At one point, the prosecutor had asked him if he understood the plea agreement. Pretty humiliating.

He checked his watch as he approached the entrance to his hotel. He'd expected a call from Manning by now, begging him to stay on the case and agreeing to accept the prosecution's offer. All Cody needed was to lose the Manning account. His partners would string him up.

The doorman in his red formal uniform opened the door for him. Cody had just gotten inside when he heard the screeching of car brakes. He looked over his shoulder and recognized Manning's Ferrari. The valet trotted toward Manning, who jumped out and threw the guy his keys.

Cody smiled, and continued through the lobby toward the elevators. A moment later, he heard Manning's loud, obnoxious voice calling him. Cody resisted the temptation to ignore him and get into the elevator, but it was much better to get the case over with. He stopped and turned.

Manning approached, clearly out of breath, his face red with exertion. The guy was only thirty and he already had a middle-age paunch. Too much booze, apparently. Pathetic. He hoped the guy got some help soon. He really did.

"Okay," Manning said brokenly, trying to catch his breath. "Let's talk about this plea agreement."

Cody nodded.

"Let's go to the bar."

He snorted. "Harrison, I know you're not that obtuse."

"I'll have coffee, okay?"

"Count on it." He led the way to a table in the corner where it was relatively private.

When the waitress came for their order, Cody promptly requested coffee for both of them, ignoring Manning's resentful look.

She'd barely walked away when Manning said, "I want you to try and get some of the community service time reduced."

"I've already tried," Cody said dryly. As he recently found out, the guy had been in enough trouble enough times that he should know the drill. "This is as good a deal as you're going to get. And trust me, it's a damn good one. The civil settlement is another matter."

"I don't care about that, he'll get his damn money." Manning glared off into space, his expression twisted and calculating.

Cody fought to keep his mouth shut. He wasn't here to judge. But it was getting so bad that after just two days, it was hard to even look at the guy.

The pianist started playing across the lounge, drawing Cody's attention.

That's when he saw her.

Sara.

With a man, sitting near the baby grand piano.

Vaguely, Cody heard Manning talking but he didn't catch what he'd said. The woman had to be Sara, yet she looked so different. Her hair not so much, but the sexy way she was dressed, with a low-cut neckline and bared shoulders, was a total contradiction. Even the flirty way she crossed one leg over the other and slowly swung it wasn't Sara.

"Shea, it's my ass that's on the line. Are you listening?"

"What?"

"What are you looking at?" Manning started to turn around.

"Nothing." Cody quickly focused on Manning. "What have you decided?"

"I won't contest the amount of community service but I want a guarantee that they don't put me in an orange vest and make me pick up trash off I75."

"You're not in a position to bargain. You're already getting off easy."

Sara didn't dress like that with him. She didn't wear skirts that short. She wasn't even the type. And who was the guy? Hell, she was supposed to be at a business dinner.

"You think my father's going to put up with that? Having me publicly humiliated?"

Cody laughed to himself. What a piece of work Manning was. He didn't mind humiliating himself with public intoxication. But Cody wisely decided not to point that out. He needed to be done with him, though. All he cared about was finding out what Sara was doing here and why she'd lied to him. But how would he do that? Walk up to her? Watch her squirm? Not his style.

Manning kept running his mouth about the importance of his family. Cody pretended to listen. He was even tempted to order Manning a double shot of Wild Turkey. The hundred-and-one-proof liquor would shut him up for a while. For what? So Cody could watch Sara flirt with another man?

Several other men stopped at her table, in fact, it seemed she knew a good many people, customers and employees alike. An idea formed, one he didn't like, but the evidence pointed in that direction. The high class escort business was big money and Sara needed... He shook his head. That was crazy. That wasn't the Sara he knew. But neither was the image in front of him.

The waitress put a cup of coffee on the table, momentarily blocking his view of Sara. But he could still see the guy she was with, could see how the man smiled at her and leaned close, the way he touched her arm with familiarity. When the waitress moved away, Cody watched Sara put her hand on the guy's thigh.

The scene made him sick. He had to get out of here. Up to his room. Be alone, and lick his wounds. But it all came down to one question—who was the real Sara Wells?

SARA SET the candles she'd bought on the coffee table, along with a vase of fresh flowers, and then she perched on the cushioned window seat overlooking the street. She wouldn't light the French vanilla-scented candles until she saw Cody's cab pull up.

She was way too nervous to do anything else. He'd sounded so peculiar on the phone. For a moment, she thought he didn't want to come over. So of course she had to replay every minute of last night in her head and obsess on every detail. For the life of her, she couldn't figure out what had gone wrong. For her, their time together had been incredible. Perfect. It didn't even matter that they'd only gotten four hours of sleep.

At five-thirty when he got up to leave, he clearly hadn't wanted to go, and she'd been a breath away from begging him to come back to bed. Promising him anything if he'd just stay with her another hour. She'd felt so safe and wanted, curled up against his warm, hard body. He'd been surprisingly unselfish. She hadn't expected him to be so attentive to her needs. So giving, and asking for nothing in return. That hadn't stopped her, though. She'd given as good as she got.

She hoped. Maybe he'd been disappointed. Or maybe...the thought that the chase was over and he'd lost interest struck her like a bolt of lightning. That's why he didn't sound enthusiastic about coming over tonight. The idea twisted a knot in her gut. He was probably coming to tell her not to bother him anymore.

Out of the window she saw the cab pull up. She watched him get out, aware of his labored movements, as if he were about to do something he didn't want to face. She shouldn't have called him. She should have waited for him to call, and if he didn't, forget about him. Right. As if she could forget last night.

She stayed huddled at the window until she heard him knock. It took her a moment to compose herself and then she went to the door, leaving the candles unlit. She shouldn't have been surprised when she opened the door but…

"Oh, my." She stared at his affected eye. "It's really black and blue."

"Yes, it is."

"I've never seen a black eye in person."

"You have now." He ran his gaze down the front of her simple blue blouse, down to her white capris and then to her gold sandals. Almost as if he didn't want to make eye contact, he looked past her into the apartment.

"Oh, come in." Her heart picked up speed. Maybe the black eye was the reason for his odd mood. Not her. She thought about kissing him, but nixed the idea. Better to let him make the next move. "Are you hungry?"

"I thought you had a business dinner."

"I did, but I picked up some takeout and wine on the way home in case you hadn't eaten."

His gaze went to the flowers and candles. He didn't even smile. "How was your meeting?"

"Boring. I thought it would never end. Why don't you sit down? I'll get you a glass of wine." She wished she weren't so nervous. But he hadn't smiled once since he'd arrived. The tension was as thick as the ninety percent humidity outside.

"I'm surprised you called." He had on gray suit pants and a white dress shirt, the two top buttons unfastened, but no coat or tie.

"I said I would." From the kitchen she could see him sit on the far side of the couch. He almost looked angry. She opened a bottle of merlot, which she knew he preferred, and proceeded to spill more than what ended up in his glass.

He didn't say anything, and she didn't try to continue the conversation until she brought their wine into the living room with her. Dammit. Her hand shook when she passed him his glass. He definitely noticed. That gave him an opening, but he still didn't say a word.

She sat beside him on the couch but at a respectable distance, wanting to ask if she'd done something wrong. But that sounded so pathetic. So she did the next best thing. She set down her glass on the coffee table, leaned over and kissed him.

Initially he was reluctant. But it took only a second for his lips to soften and then his mouth to open. Far from gentle, he kissed her back. Deep.

Urgent. The kiss was different…he was different from last night.

She was the first to pull back. They stared at each other for a long torturous moment, the look of disappointment in his eyes a total mystery.

"Tell me what's wrong," she said finally.

Anger glinted in his eyes. "You lied to me."

"About what?"

One eyebrow went up. "Where were you tonight?"

"I already told you."

"Where was the dinner?"

Her own annoyance started to burgeon. "At the Four Seasons, not that it's any of your business."

He slowly shook his head, the disappointment back in his face. "I saw you, Sara."

"Where?"

He gave her a patronizing look, and paused long enough to push another button. "At the Ritz-Carlton."

She frowned. "I haven't been there since before I went to New York."

"Whoever you're seeing, clearly it's your business. What I object to is you lying to me and wasting my time."

"Wasting your time?" Sara's temper rose another notch. She'd realized what had happened, but that was no longer the point. "Explain that to me. Wait. First, tell me what exactly you think I was doing at the Ritz?"

His expression wavered, and for the first time he seemed unsure of himself. "You're an attractive woman. You probably have men lining up to spend time with you."

"And?"

"You do the math."

"No, spell it out." She wasn't about to let him off the hook on this one. No way in hell.

"Look, I saw you with that guy."

"No," she said sweetly, getting to her feet. If she had the strength to bodily throw him out, she'd seriously consider it. "You saw my sister, Shelby. And I assure you, she doesn't have them line up, either."

8

NOT FOR A SECOND did Cody mistake the anger in Sara's face. He didn't blame her. He felt like hell. "You didn't tell me you had a twin."

"You didn't tell me you were such a moron."

He gave her a self-deprecating smile. "I thought you would've figured that one out by yourself."

Her expression softened. "Maybe I overreacted. You're not the first one to mistake me for Shelby."

"Even for twins, you two look remarkably alike." Except for the clothes. Sexy, yet chic. The hair was different, too, now that he stopped to think about it. Same length and color, but still different.

She sat down again. "However, you are the first to mistake either of us for a hooker."

He sighed. How he'd ever arrived at that conclusion was unfathomable. Granted, he didn't know Sara that well, but certainly well enough. "My apologies."

Sara smiled. "I will have to tell Shelby. About a second after I introduce you."

"Thanks," he said dryly, uncertain how he felt about the fact that she wanted him to meet any of her family. "Can you use escort and not hooker?"

"Oh, right. Much better."

"I don't suppose you'd skip the commentary altogether."

"Not a chance. Don't worry. She'll think it's hysterical."

"When did she get back from Europe?"

"Around noon. She called me last night and told me she was on her way."

"Ah, the secretive phone call you got at dinner."

She gave him a dirty look. "There was nothing secretive about it. I had to go outside so I could hear."

He might have believed her if she hadn't suddenly looked away, as if she feared her eyes might reveal too much.

So she had something to hide. What did he care? He'd probably see her a couple more times before he headed back to New York, and that would be it. Sara was really a terrific woman, but there was no future for them.

Eventually he'd get married, but one thing was certain—his potential spouse would have to be well-connected and above reproach. Simple as that, because he couldn't rule politics out of his future.

She looked back at him and slowly smiled. "Do you know that this is the first time I've seen you without a suit on?"

"How quickly you've forgotten last night?"

"You know what I mean," she said, her cheeks turning pink. "Although that was a pretty good look for you." Any hint of embarrassment was instantly gone and she moved closer to unbutton his shirt. "I'd really like another preview."

He leaned back, stretching his arm along the back of the couch and watched her slip each button free. Instead of urging him out of the shirt, she went straight for his belt. That was all he needed to start getting hard. He saw the corners of her mouth twitch.

"You must have a thing for this couch." He tensed when she unzipped his fly.

"Nope. I want to talk. If we go straight to bed, that won't happen."

"Right. This is conducive to talking." He jerked when she slid a finger into the opening of his boxers and had to evade her hand.

"Okay." She sat back and folded her hands in her lap.

"Do I have an option here? I'm seriously talked out today."

She looked curiously at him, and then her eyes lit with understanding. "Oh, your case. Is it settled?"

"Not sure."

"Weren't you discussing a plea agreement?"

"We were."

"You're going to court?"

"I hope not." Dealing with the likes of Manning had been an eye-opener. It wasn't easy defending someone like him, no matter that Cody truly believed in the law and that everyone deserved a defense. "What do you look so pleased about?"

"It would mean you'd stay longer," she said, smiling.

Her honesty took him by surprise. He didn't know

how to comment. The thing was, he wasn't ready to say goodbye to her, either. That idea alone should have sent him running back to Manhattan.

"So, tell me about the case."

"I can't do that."

"Oh. Right. Sorry." She seemed genuinely disappointed, then she smiled. "Okay then. Tell me a secret," she said, and when he frowned, she added, "Nothing huge. Just something you wouldn't normally talk about."

That silenced him. He didn't talk to women. Not like that, anyway. The ones he dated talked about the latest play, or about upcoming charity balls and fashion shows. They knew he was a prominent, highly paid attorney who'd graduated from Harvard and came from an upper-middle-class family, and that seemed to be enough for them.

"I hate to disappoint you," he finally said, "but there are no skeletons in my closet."

"I didn't mean that kind of secret. Something more generic, but that you wouldn't necessarily discuss with anyone at work." She obviously wasn't giving up; maybe it was his imagination, but she seemed to move farther away from him with each word.

Cody huffed. "This is blackmail."

"Sue me." She grinned, and he realized he was going to give in.

"All right, this is something only my sister Dallas knows, and maybe Dakota, too."

"Yes?"

"Remember I told you that I played baseball in high school and college?"

She nodded, but looked dubious that he was about to offer anything worthwhile. She was in for a surprise.

"I wanted to play pro ball."

Her eyes widened. "You?"

"I did."

"What stopped you? An injury?" Her gaze ran down his body as if looking for something she might have missed.

"My parents."

At the indignation that flashed in Sara's eyes, warmth spread throughout his chest. "How?"

"They didn't see any future in sports. They wanted me to go to law school." Actually, they found sports an indignity, but he decided to leave that out. It was done. And they were right. He was successful and needn't worry about an uncertain future.

"You don't seem the type to be led by the nose."

That remark he could have done without. "I realized they were right."

"And you don't have any regrets?"

He hesitated. Too long. He saw the pity in her eyes. It pissed him off.

She took his hand. "For the record, they were probably right. You've had such a brilliant career because you're a born lawyer. If you had turned pro, now that you're thirty-five it would be tough. Younger players would be edging you out and unless you'd risen to the top, you wouldn't have any endorsements to fall back on. You'd probably end up lending your name to car dealerships. I can't imagine you doing that, can you?"

The serious and logical way she presented her assessment astonished him. But not just that, she looked adamant that he not regret his career path. Her concern felt oddly nice. "Sounds like you know something about this."

She shrugged a shoulder. "On the other hand, I hate that your parents didn't encourage your dream."

This time, he shrugged. "My dad's a judge and my mom's a biology professor and head of her department." He smiled dismissively. "They didn't want a jock for a son."

"Don't blow it off. I can tell it bothers you. And it should. They had their lives. This one's yours."

"You're wrong. It doesn't bother me," he said, touched by her earnestness. She wasn't wrong but it was a moot point. History. Besides, she couldn't understand the pressure he'd experienced with upwardly mobile parents who wanted the best for their three children. He wasn't blind or stupid. He realized they'd sometimes been myopic in their views, but he never doubted they had his best interest at heart.

"I guess it's a universal problem. I'm having a little trouble with my parents' vision for my life, too."

He was with her parents on that one. She was too bright not to be more focused.

"And Shelby?"

Sara laughed softly. "She's a free spirit, so she pretty much gets a pass."

"Doesn't she work?"

"Technically, no."

Cody frowned. He had questions that were none of his business. But somehow, the conversation so far made him appreciate his parents more. They'd provided him and his sisters with good educations that offered them options. That Sara was content to work as a temp was a damn shame. She was too bright and talented. "What do your parents do?"

Her lips lifted in a reluctant smile and she paused, as if deciding what to say. "My dad owns his own business. Mom's never worked."

"What kind of business?"

"Cotton manufacturing, among other things. Would you like some more wine?" She got up before he answered and hurried to the kitchen.

But not before he'd noticed her watch. That's when realization struck. The expensive purse and shoes, the exclusive prep school, the simple but pricey Cartier around her wrist that cost more than some people's cars. The reluctance to talk about herself or where she'd gone to college. Working as a temp and sharing an apartment with a roommate. It all made sense now.

Her family had had money once, but it had run out. He'd seen it before. The nouveau riche who'd acquired a windfall and, instead of investing, blew it all in a matter of years. The problem was, that made women like her dangerous, constantly seeking what they'd lost.

Still, as he watched her come back to the couch, an expensive bottle of merlot in her hand, he just couldn't see it. Sara wasn't that type of woman. Maybe he was right about the family losing money, but she was the exception, content to live in a modest apartment and look until she found the right job.

After she refilled each of their glasses, he asked, "Since your father owns his own business, why aren't you working for him?"

She took a quick sip of wine. "Really sore subject." Shaking her head, she set down her glass. "That's a decision I have to make soon."

"Yeah, the whole family dynamic is tough enough, but working side by side…" He couldn't imagine working with either of his parents.

She opened her mouth to say something and then closed it again.

"What?"

"It's complicated, and frankly, I don't think you would understand."

"Thanks for the vote of confidence."

"No offense. It's dumb family stuff. Anyway…" She cupped him over his fly, immediately getting his attention. "Did you really want to talk all night?"

"You're going to pay for that."

"I hope so."

"Come here." He got up and pulled her to her feet. He'd forgotten his belt was unbuckled; his trousers unsnapped, and he had to do some quick maneuvering to keep them up.

Sara started laughing, and he abandoned his plan to get her to the bedroom and started undressing her right where she stood.

"Wait." She turned toward the open window blinds, but he backed up, bringing her with him and continuing to rid her of her blouse and bra. They made it to the kitchen and he slid down her capris. She stepped out of them, leaving them piled on the floor.

He slid off her panties, crouching down to kiss the soft, springy hair at the juncture of her thighs. Her musky scent robbed him of rationale. He molded his hands over her firm backside and pulled her against his mouth. Shivering, she pushed her fingers through his hair. The position was wrong. He couldn't reach her like he wanted.

He got up and lifted her onto the counter a little too roughly and spread her thighs. She didn't resist, didn't even seem surprised. He used his finger first, so he could also taste her ripened breasts. She was so wet, so ready for him, it was going to take all of his willpower not to strip off the rest of his clothes and lay her back, slide his cock into the silky slickness.

Her ragged breathing made her breasts rise and fall, and he touched each nipple lightly with the tip of his tongue, teasing her but making himself insane. He took one crown into his mouth and suckled hard until she moaned and tried to touch him. He couldn't let her. Once she did, the last shred of his control would snap.

What was it about this woman that made him want to please her? He'd been accused of being a selfish bastard more than once. He'd never denied it. But with Sara he felt different. No explaining the sudden transformation. The feeling would fade, of course. It had to.

CLOSING HER EYES, Sara clutched his shoulders. She wanted his shirt off but she didn't want him to stop what he was doing. She didn't want to think about where she was sitting, totally naked, in Chloe's kitchen. She simply wanted to enjoy the feel of his tongue slipping in between the folds and touching that oh-so-sensitive spot.

He stopped for a moment and gently pried her hands from his shoulders. Confused, she opened her eyes. He kissed her briefly on the lips and then put her hands on the counter at an angle behind her so that she was leaning backward. Her thighs still spread, he pulled her hips toward him so that she was fully exposed. He lowered his mouth again, spreading the folds apart with his fingers, and using his tongue to do wickedly delicious things to her clit.

Once his mouth was positioned where he wanted it, he moved one hand to her right breast and played with her nipple. She couldn't help writhing but he stayed with her, pressing his mouth harder against her, his tongue firm and unerring.

She didn't want to come yet. She wanted it to last longer, but she didn't have a choice. The spasms came, over and over, wave after wave of sensation as unrelenting as Cody's practiced tongue. She tried not to cry out; her lip stung from being clamped under her teeth. Finally she let go of the counter and stifled a scream.

Cody slowed down but she finally had to push him away. His mouth was damp, his nostrils flared and his pupils were so dilated his eyes looked black.

Their eyes met for a moment and then he looked back down where his fingers continued to explore. She should have been nervous that everything was right there for his inspection. Oddly, she wasn't.

"Okay," she said finally, her voice so hoarse she barely recognized it. "My turn."

"I'm not finished."

She shoved him backward, catching him off guard. When he stumbled, she slid off the counter. As soon as he righted himself, he removed his cuff links and she pushed the shirt off his shoulders. She smiled when he let the expensive custom-made shirt fall to the floor and then ignored it. His white T-shirt nearly ripped when they both grabbed the hem at the same time. But he got rid of that, too, while she again unbuckled his belt. His trousers landed on the gray tiled floor next to his shirt, as did his socks.

His arousal strained against the brown silk boxers, and she lightly traced him through the satiny fabric. Goose bumps popped out on his chest, and he shuddered.

She lowered her hands. "Now, you're coming with me." At this point she knew she wouldn't get an argument, so she immediately turned around and headed for the bedroom, knowing he would follow. When they reached their destination, he was wearing a smile she hadn't seen before. Kind of sexy, kind of cocky, kind of heart-melting.

"This is my court, counselor, my rules. And the first thing we do is take those off." She sat at the edge of the bed, looking purposely at the boxers. Or rather the tent he'd made.

"Yes, your honor." His smile turned a little lop-sided and his gaze stayed on her, at least until he got his boxers down to his thighs. After that, she didn't know because she could only look at one thing. He was hard and smooth and incredibly ready, and damn if it didn't get her juices flowing again.

"Come here," she ordered, wishing she'd sounded more authoritative instead of breathless.

In no hurry, he moved toward her, stopping at arm's length.

"Closer."

He smiled and did as she asked.

She touched the tip of his penis, and spread around the bead of moisture that had formed. Then she gave it a quick flick of her tongue and saw his belly tighten. She circled her hand around his shaft and brought him to her lips. She sucked just the head of his cock as she licked him. His reaction, a gasp and a body jerk, told her to remember this move. She wanted to do everything he loved, but she wanted to discover those things on her own. She smiled around him. This was a fact-finding mission, and she was the perfect gal for the job.

"You're laughing?" he asked, clearly wounded. "Now?"

Still holding him, she pulled back just a hair. "Don't you worry, all's well. You relax, while I do my best to make you squeal."

He laughed, too, but that was cut short as she

sucked him back into her eager mouth, this time a lot farther. She wasn't finished with her tongue, however, and she found his sweet spot, the little ridge under the crown. Sweet, indeed, if his moans were anything to go by.

It seemed hard to believe this was actually her, that she was sitting on the bed stark naked, not thinking about how she wanted to cover up, not thinking much about herself at all, except for how to please this man.

She used her hand to pump his shaft as she enjoyed the feel of his smooth cock. He was thick, but not enough to make her jaw hurt, and he was just a few inches longer than she could comfortably take, at least in this position. Altogether wonderful, like the rest of him.

He touched the side of her face with the back of his hand. She opened her eyes to find him staring at her with a new kind of desperation in his eyes.

"I hate to say this, but you're going to have to stop that."

She pulled away, letting him go with her hand, too. "You liked it, though, right?"

"Too much," he said as he sat down next to her on the edge of the bed. "I have so much more I want to do with you."

She grinned. "Such as?"

He pulled her into a blistering kiss. She tasted sex and felt his heat, and she didn't care what he did to her as long as he did it soon.

When he broke it off, it was only to stand, to go

by the side of the bed and take her with him. She scurried onto the covers and he joined her, picking up the kiss where he'd left off.

She liked this better. Feeling his body pressing against hers. His hand moved down her side, stroking, comforting.

When she opened her eyes he was looking right into them. "You're amazing," he whispered. It wasn't a compliment, it was a discovery.

"I'm flattered."

"I'm not kidding," he said. "This is... I don't know. I didn't expect this."

"What?"

He shook his head. "Nothing. I don't know. I can't..."

"We fit," she said.

His eyes closed. When they opened again, he smiled. "Yeah."

"So enjoy it."

"I'm helpless to do anything else."

She kissed the tip of his nose. "You're many things, Cody Shea, but helpless isn't one of them."

"Around you? I'm not so sure."

She snuggled closer. "For the record, I find you amazing right back."

He lifted her chin with the side of his finger. "Amazing."

"Did I mention that I'm also very flexible?"

His grin made her shiver. And then she couldn't do anything but go along for the ride.

THEY BOTH laid there, still touching at the hip, but too exhausted to move. After a few minutes, with Herculean effort, Sara rolled over and flopped her arm across his chest. He smiled and stroked her hair.

She'd come to a decision. She'd been evasive about her personal life, and it had to be obvious to him. No telling what he thought about her. And she had no idea what the truth would change between them. But at this point, hadn't he proven himself? To him she was Sara Wells, a temporary worker who had nothing to offer him. He wasn't after her money, or her family's influence. They'd gotten along better than she'd ever dreamed. Even though she'd put him through a few hoops in the past couple of days, he'd come out shining. For the old Cody, the black eye alone would've been the final blow. But she was finding that there was so much more to him, and she couldn't wait to peel away the layers. She had nothing to lose. Tomorrow she'd tell him everything. And she knew how she'd do it, too.

"Do you ever wear jeans?"

He brought his head up to look at her. "Yes," he said blandly.

"Have a pair with you?"

"Why?"

"I have a surprise for you tomorrow night."

He shook his head.

Her heart sank, and she started to shrink away. They'd had mind-blowing sex, but had she assumed too much? Was this it? Was he getting on a plane tomorrow? "I promise you'll like it."

"I already have plans for us."

Relieved, she twirled her fingers through the smattering of hair on his chest. "What?"

"You'll find out tomorrow."

"But—"

"Have I, or have I not been a good sport about letting you call the shots?" he asked.

"Yes, but—"

"I'm sure your surprise can wait until Thursday."

"Well—"

Then he kissed her soundly. There would be no discussion. She wasn't crazy about the idea, but it would be poor form to back out. Besides, how could she think when his hand was again sliding up her thigh? She only hoped tomorrow night wouldn't backfire.

9

BAREFOOT AND STILL WEARING her short strappy silk nightgown, Shelby frowned at the inside of the sparse stainless steel refrigerator. "Want me to take your place tonight?"

"No. Absolutely not." They'd done that before, just like every other set of twins. But not since prep school. And certainly not this time. The thought of Cody and Shelby together? Unbearable.

"Sounds serious, *mi amora*."

"I hate it when you do that."

"What?"

"Every time you come back from another country you have to use every new word you know a hundred times."

Shelby turned around. "Sensitive, aren't we?"

Ignoring her, Sara shook her head at the amazing amount of clutter on the kitchen countertops. Already, their apartment was a mess. Boxes of Belgian and Swiss chocolates, bottles of perfume and two cases of French wine covered the granite. "You've been home for only one day and look at this place."

Shelby closed the door and picked up one of the

boxes of chocolate. "I sure hope you get laid to-night."

"Funny." Sara checked the wine to make sure none needed to be temperature controlled. She told Shelby almost everything, but this was off limits. No way would she tell her sister the details about the last few nights with Cody. Just thinking about the scene in the kitchen almost made Sara drop a bottle of obscenely expensive perfume. "I'm putting the wine in the pantry. You get rid of the perfume."

"Forget the wine, what about this guy?" Shelby ripped open one of the boxes, selected a chocolate and then passed the box to Sara.

It was only nine in the morning, but what the hell. This wouldn't be the first odd thing she'd done this week. She made two chocolate selections and then carried her coffee to the totally impractical frosted glass kitchen table Shelby had insisted upon.

Shelby brought the box with her and plopped down opposite Sara. Even with her hair a tangled mess and makeup smudged under her eyes, Shelby looked gorgeous. It wasn't fair. Especially since they were identical twins. "Tell me everything. Where you met. What he does. What he looks like…"

"He's the lawyer from New York—"

Shelby put down the dark chocolate she'd bitten into. "New York?"

"Yes, he's the guy I mentioned before." In fact, she kind of hoped Shelby had forgotten.

"Hmm. Guess he was interested, after all."

"Not really. He's here on business."

"But he's seen you every night, yes?"

"Well, yeah."

"So explain why you don't want to go to La Maisonette tonight. You know their escargot is to die for."

Sara cleared her throat. "I haven't exactly told him everything about me."

Shelby soberly held Sara's gaze, and nodded. If anyone understood, she did. Even more than their parents. "Is he someone you would tell?"

"Yes, eventually," Sara said slowly.

Shelby planted her elbows on the table and leaned forward. "He's special, huh?"

"He's not supposed to be."

Shelby smiled. "It's about time."

"Don't get excited. It's really complicated."

"Only if you let it be."

"No, seriously." Sara took a deep breath. "Cody is sort of, well, he's kind of a snob."

Shelby's mouth opened, but it took her a moment before she said, "I would have expected you to bring home a gorilla first."

"He's not that bad. I shouldn't have used that word." The truth was, though, the Cody she'd known in New York had been a snob. He'd changed some, but she didn't fool herself. It wasn't as if he'd take her home to his parents. Not as she was portraying herself now, anyway.

"This isn't good," Shelby said in a serious tone, shaking her head. "What kind of money does he have?"

"I don't know. He does all right."

"What happens when he finds out our family has more money than God?"

"I hate it when you say it like that." Sara got up and went to the coffeepot.

"It's true. Whether you like it or not."

"You want some?" She held up the pot to her sister.

"Listen to me. He might even know who you are. Have you thought about that?"

"He doesn't."

"How do you know?"

"I just know."

Shelby clearly wasn't convinced. She sat back, concern pulling her brows together in a frown. "You swore Robert didn't know, either."

"I was nineteen." Almost eight years later, Sara could feel the shame and humiliation. Robert had been charming and fun and showered her with silly gifts that made her laugh. She'd fallen hard, at least as hard as a foolish nineteen-year-old could fall.

But all of it had been about the money. Shelby had stepped in and proven that by pretending to seduce Robert. He'd eagerly taken the bait with the promise that they'd run off with Shelby's trust fund.

The lesson had been huge. After that, Sara had rarely dated. And when she had, it had been casual, never allowing the relationship to last more than three or four months. She'd been content and safe. But then she'd met Cody, and safety wasn't good enough. Damn him.

"I just thought of something." Shelby tapped one

of her long red fingernails on the glass top. "There's no way he could've gotten a reservation at La Maisonette. Not since he's been here. There's usually a month's waiting list."

"But he'd know that. Maybe the hotel concierge got him in."

Shelby made a face. "Possibly, if the tip was big enough."

"Great." Sara's hopes plummeted again. She went back to the table and sank into her chair. "I don't know. Maybe this is for the best. Let him find out tonight. It's not as if I haven't given him enough hints."

"Sweetie, there aren't enough hints to describe how—"

Sara held up a hand. "Please, do not use the phrase 'more money than God.'"

"Thank you. You said it for me." Shelby laughed at the nasty look Sara gave her, then pushed the box of chocolates toward her. "Here. This will make everything better."

"Right."

"Tell you what. Big sister will take care of everything," Shelby said, and Sara threw a napkin at her. That was the second thing Shelby always said that Sara hated. Jeez, they'd only been born a minute apart. "If he did manage to get a reservation, I'll talk to Mario and have him cancel it."

Shelby threw back the napkin. Anticipating the move, grinning, Sara caught it. She was so glad Shelby was home. She always knew what to do.

AFTER SARA LEFT to meet a prospective employer for lunch, Shelby got out her laptop. It took a little doing but she'd teased out enough information from Sara about Cody that Shelby could do some checking on her own. She'd gotten pretty good at it. Any guy she dated more than three times got checked out. If they made it to two months, she had a very reputable private detective she used for background checks.

Sara would be totally appalled, but that was because she was too naive. Good thing she didn't date much. Shelby had enough of her own problems with men who turned out to be lying jerks.

The law firm Cody Shea worked for was top-notch and made up mostly of Harvard graduates. His parents were respectable professionals who, along with Cody, often ended up in the society pages. That wasn't always a good thing, though not necessarily bad, either.

Mostly they were associated with charities, that of course being a plus. But Shelby and Sara knew too many upwardly mobile people who used that circuit to hobnob with the rich and famous. Which type was Cody?

Shelby leaned back and stared idly at the screen. A computer wasn't going to tell her that. It didn't bode well that Sara had already said he was a snob. He wasn't even wealthy enough to be nouveau riche, and those people could annoy the hell out of her. There was only one thing to do. She had to meet this guy, although Sara wouldn't like it. She'd probably refuse, even if Shelby promised to be on her best behavior.

She thought for a minute and then, smiling, reached for the phone. After all, she'd promised Sara she'd call La Maisonette's maître d'. After two rings, the lunch hostess answered and forwarded the call.

"Mario? It's Shelby Wellington. Listen, darlin', I need a favor."

DAKOTA HAD already wasted half the morning wallowing in indecision. Sara hadn't posted any more on Eve's Apple, and Dakota hadn't heard from her brother. If she expected to get any work done, she simply had to pick up the phone. Case closed.

She got Cody after the third ring. "Hey. Busy?"

"Frustrated."

"The case?"

"Manning's an asshole."

Dakota blinked. That did not sound like her brother. With clients, he usually had the patience of a saint. "What's going on?"

"The guy has more money than brains. He's a drunk, and he expects a free pass."

"He's not open to a plea agreement?"

"As long as the deal is on his terms." Lowering his voice, he added, "He needs to go to rehab. Or jail."

Dakota took a second to process. The Mannings were a huge account. This wasn't like Cody. She hoped no one heard that remark. "Where are you?"

"We've been talking to the D.A. but Manning's downstairs having a cigarette."

"What's your gut telling you? Think you'll be able to wrap things up today?"

He didn't say anything for a long time. "Why? What's going on?"

"Nothing. This isn't even an official call."

"Then what?"

"Bite my head off, why don't you?"

"Sorry, just tired."

She hesitated…maybe now wasn't the time. Oh, what the hell. "Hope it's Sara keeping you up late and not work."

"Goodbye, Dakota."

"Wait!" Too late. He'd hung up.

She replaced the receiver on the cradle, angry at first. But then she smiled. Cody would never have hung up on her if she hadn't hit a sore spot and she knew from Sara's post that they'd seen each other. But were things good between them? How would she even find out?

Laying her head against the back of her leather chair, she stared at the Monet print on her office wall. How could she help yet not be intrusive? She ached for her brother. She'd never seen him truly happy. No, he'd been happier when she was in middle school and he was a freshman in college. She'd gone to one of his baseball games with her parents. His home run had won the game, and he'd been carried off the field.

She hadn't known much about baseball, still didn't, but the joy on her brother's face had her on her feet and cheering along with everyone else. But not her parents. They'd applauded with the rest of the crowd, but it was clear they'd been upset. Cody had seen it, too. That single event changed her attitude toward her brother.

When they were younger, she and Dallas had had a love-hate relationship with him. He'd always been the good son, the one who effortlessly got straight A's, the one who was most likely to succeed, as the saying went.

Not that any of the Shea children had a choice. They attended excellent schools and were burdened with high expectations. But Cody never had a chance. They'd always been hardest on him. They still were. Dallas had openly rebelled. By choosing Tony, Dakota had quietly done the same. Now everything rode on Cody. He was the family star, the one who could end up in the State building, maybe even in Congress.

She loved her parents. She did. They meant well. But they'd been too damn hard on their children. Did Cody even see that? Was he happy dating the socialite du jour? She knew most of those women. They weren't right for him. They didn't even care about him, only about what he could afford to give them. Sara wasn't like that. She could make him happy. Dakota was certain of it.

She checked the crystal Mikasa clock on her credenza. Seeing that she still had a few minutes, she quickly logged on the Eve's Apple Web site, and started to type.

Dear Sara…

SARA HEARD the doorbell and smoothed the front of the simple black dress that would have been appropriate for La Maisonette, but just as suitable anywhere they ended up. She knew it was Cody but out of habit she peered out of Chloe's apartment door peephole. His eye was still black and blue, and she had to give him credit for still wanting to go out.

"You look beautiful," he said as soon as she opened the door, his gaze running down the front of her dress to the black open-toed heels that she'd bought this afternoon.

"You look pretty good yourself."

"Yeah." He gingerly touched the corner of his eye.

She grabbed his yellow silk tie and tugged him toward her. "We can always stay in."

"Tempting, but…"

She silenced him with a blistering kiss that had them both stumbling back into the apartment. He cupped her bottom and hauled her against him. Already he was getting hard.

His hands slackened and he slowly pulled away. "We can't start this."

"Why not?" She drew the back of her hand down over the bulging fabric.

He stiffened and inhaled sharply. "Because I promised you a nice dinner."

"I don't care about dinner." She moved her hand so she could get close and rubbed her hips against him. "We can eat any time."

He groaned. "Do you know what I went through to get our reservation?"

Guilt assailed her. But just for a moment. She had to look at the bigger picture. "You must be getting old if you'd let dinner stop you."

"Man, right below the belt."

She laughed. "That's where I'm aiming."

"Later," he said, moving her away. "We have a cab waiting."

A STRING OF imported cars lined up, awaiting the busy valet parkers. Behind them was another line of limos, their drivers either standing outside talking or reading magazines behind the wheel as they waited. On any given night, La Maisonette was crowded, but tonight it seemed as if half of Atlanta had decided to show up for dinner. Sara was bound to see someone she knew.

Their cab pulled to the curb, and she fought the urge to instruct the driver to wait so they could get out of here as quickly as possible. Of course she couldn't, because then Cody would know she'd been involved in canceling the reservation.

As soon as she got out of the cab, she saw a valet parker she recognized and, of course, the doorman. They also recognized her. She gave them each a brief smile and turned her head so that they wouldn't address her.

Shelby's plan had sounded so good this morning. Too good. This was totally foolish, and Sara should have known better. "I'll meet you in the restaurant," she told him as soon as she stepped foot on the Persian rug in the lobby. "I need to go to the ladies' room."

Before he could respond, she ducked behind the massive urn of fresh flowers that stood in the middle of the lobby. The tall arrangement with its orange and yellow gladiolus and lavender sprays gave her cover until she could make it to the other side. Mario and the wait staff would recognize her. After Cody found out they had no reservation, she'd meet him on the way out.

On the burgundy velvet couch in the ladies' room foyer sat two older women that, luckily, Sara didn't know. She smiled at them and then hurried around the corner. At the gilded mirror, Abigail Van De Veer, Sara's mother's longtime friend, applied pink lipstick.

Sara froze, unsure if she should dart into a stall or exchange a few pleasantries and hope the woman wouldn't ask too many questions.

"Well, well, I haven't seen you in a good long while." Cornelia, a permanent fixture who'd passed out towels in the ladies' room for as long as Sara could remember, hurried toward her, wiping her palms on her ruffled white apron.

At that, Mrs. Van De Veer turned toward Sara. "Your mother told me you were back in town," she said, tucking the lipstick into her slim silver evening bag.

Cornelia immediately backed up when Mrs. Van De Veer cut her off. Sara gave the older black woman an apologetic look. It was embarrassing how some of the women treated her as if she were part of the gold embossed wallpaper. They barely looked at her as she handed them towels for their wet hands, and then ignored her as they tossed a dollar into the silver plate on the counter.

"How are you, Mrs. Van De Veer?" Sara asked politely. "I hear you're busy with Miranda's wedding plans." The words were barely out of her mouth when Sara realized her error.

"True," Mrs. Van De Veer began, "and if I told you all the trouble I've had with caterers and florists and…"

Sara quit listening as the woman complained at length. On the plus side, she wasn't getting any questions directed at her, and by now Cody would be waiting outside the door. Unfortunately, he was probably about to send someone in after her.

"Excuse me, Mrs. Van De Veer," she finally said, and pointed to a stall. "I really have to make a visit."

"Oh, heavens. Go. Go." She waved her hand. "Maybe you'll join your mother and me for tea sometime."

"Absolutely. Nice seeing you." Sara disappeared into the stall, sat down and waited. She counted off a minute in her head, flushed, and then slowly opened the door. Thankfully, no one else had come in.

"So, how have you and your husband been?" she asked Cornelia as she went to the sink to wash her hands.

"We've been doing just fine, Ms. Wellington. Thanks for askin'." She waited beside Sara, promptly handing her a towel after she turned off the gold-plated faucet. "Have you been away lately?"

"Yes, but I'm home for good now." She dropped

the usual ten-dollar tip in the woman's plate. Her husband, a heart patient, hadn't worked in five years and she knew they had to be struggling. "How can you always tell me from Shelby?"

Cornelia smiled and shrugged her plump shoulders. "Anyway, today I cheated. Shelby's already been in here."

Sara frowned. Cornelia had to be mistaken. "Today?"

"Maybe fifteen minutes ago."

"But...but...are you sure?" Sara's heart raced. There had to be a good explanation. Maybe Shelby had decided to take the reservation herself.

"I'm sure. She's always real nice to me, just like you."

Sara forced a smile. "You take care, Cornelia."

At the risk of seeming rude, she rushed out of the ladies' room, hoping Cody was nearby. No sign of him. She had no choice but to head toward the maître d' stand. Cody stood off to the side, holding a glass of wine. He did not look like a man who didn't have a reservation.

Had he even checked yet? Dammit. She should have known he had the good manners to wait. He spotted her and she pushed herself forward. Unfortunately, Mario saw her, too.

"Good evening, Ms. Wellington," he said, coming around the podium to kiss the back of her hand. "So wonderful to have you back."

"Thank you, Mario," she said softly. But it was too late. Cody was beside her, frowning.

"I believe we have a reservation," he said, sliding a curious look at Sara.

"Yes, of course." Mario spread a hand toward the back of the restaurant. "Please," he said. "The rest of your party has already arrived."

_10_

"I BELIEVE YOU HAVE mistaken us for someone else. The name is Shea."

"Yes, of course, Mr. Shea. Please follow me." Mario flashed his white megawatt smile and proceeded to lead them past tables covered with white linen tablecloths and set with polished silver.

"Do you know anything about this?" Cody asked, close to her ear, his hand at the small of her back.

"I'm afraid so."

"Want to enlighten me?"

Sara's laugh sounded strangled. She just kept walking, keeping her face straight ahead.

"He called you Ms. Wellington."

"I'm going to kill Shelby."

"What's going on?" he murmured. He didn't like surprises, cared even less for being left in the dark. He'd expected a quiet romantic dinner, not this.

The restaurant was intimate, elegant, tables adorned with fresh flowers and candles, but it seemed to take forever to get across. Most people didn't look up from their private conversations, but the few who did watched him and Sara with open curiosity.

"Ah, here we are." As soon as Mario stepped aside, Cody saw Sara's twin sitting at the table. "I hope this is to your liking."

The dark-haired man he'd seen with Shelby yesterday immediately stood when Mario pulled out the high-back, upholstered chair for Sara.

"Thank you, Mario," Sara said, gracefully lowering herself onto the chair and smiling at the man. She wasn't overt about it, but Cody caught the brief glare directed at her sister.

Cody had no choice but to claim the remaining seat at the table. Shelby's date sat down, and after the solicitous Mario assured them he was always available to accommodate any of their needs, he seemed to disappear into thin air.

"Where the hell did you get that shiner?" Shelby stared at him as if he'd just rolled through the mud and then had the audacity to enter sacred ground.

Sara gasped. "Shelby."

"I hope this is a really juicy story." She did look remarkably like Sara, except she wore more makeup and her fingernails were long and red, while Sara's were short, neat and with a subtle sheen to them. "By the way, this is…" She leaned toward her companion, tilting her head and pressing her shoulder to his. "This is Carlo. That's my sister, Sara."

The man gave a short bow with his head and smiled, but said nothing.

"He doesn't speak much English." With fascinated interest, Shelby turned back to Cody. "Tell me about the shiner."

"Enough, Shelby," Sara said softly. She kept her hands in her lap but he could see the slight quiver in her lips. Obviously she was displeased, and her not having been a party to this helped calm him down.

"I'm Cody Shea," he said, left to introduce himself, and Sara sent him an apologetic look. He didn't blame her; in fact, he wished he could reach her hand. Give her a squeeze. Tell her it was going to be all right. Dinner was only a small part of the evening.

Two waiters silently approached, removing Shelby and her date's empty cocktail glasses. One of them asked Sara if she'd like her usual and she nodded, looking miserable. He ordered his scotch, the earlier anger returning.

Who was this woman? She'd said her family had money, but this wasn't the kind of restaurant even the upper middle class frequented enough to have a usual. He doubted they even carried a bottle of wine for less than a hundred bucks. If the four of them could walk out for a bill under a thousand, he'd be very surprised.

"So, I guess everyone is wondering why this became a foursome." Shelby smiled, looking from him to Sara. "My instigation. I knew I'd never get to meet you, otherwise. But this is the perfect opportunity, n'est-ce pas?"

"Oh, God," Sara muttered.

Shelby laughed. "So, Cody, tell me about yourself."

"Forget it, Shelby." Sara picked up the linen napkin she'd placed on her lap. "I think we'll find someplace else to eat."

"It's okay, Sara." Cody reached over and took her hand. "I'm happy to meet your sister."

Sending Shelby a resentful look, Sara dropped the napkin back in her lap. "You won't say that in an hour."

Unfazed, Shelby focused on Cody. "You were saying?"

"I doubt there's anything to tell." Cody smiled back. "I have a feeling you already know all about me."

Shelby bubbled with laughter and glanced at Sara. "I like him already."

Sara's eyes widened at her sister, her cheeks starting to redden. "Shelby, tell me you didn't."

"Sara?" He tried to get her attention. "Sara?"

Fortunately, the waiters arrived, accomplishing something he couldn't. Sara finally turned her murderous glare away from Shelby. She politely thanked them before they left, and then took a healthy sip of what looked to be some kind of flavored martini.

Cody slid a look at Carlo, who'd been stoically silent from the beginning. In the hope that including him in the conversation might defuse the tension, Cody started to address him, but Shelby preempted him.

"Okay, I confess, he doesn't speak any English," she said. "Carlo is from Rome." She kissed his cheek and then, without missing a beat, turned back to Cody. "Any political aspirations?"

"Not at the moment."

"But you've been approached?"

No protest out of Sara this time. Instead, she turned expectantly to him.

"Yes, I have." He wasn't entirely comfortable with this line of questioning. No one knew he'd been solicited. Not even his family. He didn't need that pressure.

"I'm surprised you haven't jumped on the bandwagon. From what I read about you and your firm, you'd be perfect."

He smiled. "I have no idea how you could arrive at that conclusion."

"Well, you're good-looking enough to reel in the women voters." Shelby sighed. "Although I assure you that's not how all of us base our decisions. You went to Harvard Law School, which means you not only have the right level of education but you must have connections. You come from a good, solid family, who've been heavily involved in civil service, always a huge plus…"

The thoughtfulness in Shelby's eyes was the only thing that stopped him from putting an end to the conversation. Not that he had any intention of discussing his personal ambitions with her. But this wasn't idle curiosity, and he understood she wanted to protect her sister. He liked that about her.

In fact, there was a lot he liked about her. She seemed intelligent, definitely beautiful, sophisticated, glamorous, very much like the women he usually dated. If by chance they'd met at a party or charity dinner last week, he would've undoubtedly asked her out. But now?

She simply wasn't Sara.

The thought startled him. His chest tightened. He looked over at Sara, so quiet and beautiful in her simple black dress, and his tie felt as if it were about to strangle him.

"How old were you when you made partner?" Shelby asked.

He kept a light tone and said, "*You* should've been a lawyer."

"I am." Her brows furrowed, she looked at Sara. "No, I guess technically I'm not. I mean, I graduated from Yale Law School but I never took the bar exam. Sara said it was pretty easy, though."

Stunned, he looked over at her, but she wouldn't meet his eyes. She was a lawyer? But working as a temp? Had enough money to frequent a five-star restaurant like this? What the hell was her game?

"Of course, Sara was also second in our class, so I'm not sure how much I can believe that." Shelby laughed, obviously unaware of the sudden tension between her sister and Cody.

"Yale's okay," Cody said evenly, trying to stuff down his rising anger and hurt. Now wasn't the time to lose his temper. "But it doesn't come close to Harvard."

Shelby scoffed. "The only people who think that way are Harvard alumni."

The longstanding rivalry between the two Ivy League schools was still alive and well. "I'm of the understanding it's the other way around." He smiled at Sara, who looked down at her lap.

The coward.

He had a good mind to pump Shelby for more information. See how far he could get. If it made Sara squirm, too bad. At this point, what did he have to lose?

SHELBY SKIPPED DESSERT but ordered a Courvoisier. Dinner had been quiet and even Carlo, who barely understood what was happening, was subdued. How could he not be affected? The silence during their meal had been as thick as her housekeeper's peanut butter fudge. She'd have to make it up to him later, the poor guy. Maybe take him dancing before they went back to his room. Yet he'd probably rather skip the dancing. Go straight to bed. That's what she liked about European men. They were lovers, not talkers.

She snuck a peek at her sister. It was going to take a whole lot more to make it up to Sara. She was angry, her mouth pulled in a straight line, her eyes a fire blue, but good manners kept her from letting Shelby have it.

Sighing to herself, Shelby drained the last of her cabernet, wishing her brandy would come. How could she have known how little Sara had told him about herself? That in itself was troublesome. Shelby had gotten a clue this morning that this wasn't a one-night stand, but she had no idea Sara was this serious about the guy, whether she'd admit it or not.

But was he worthy?

Sara was special. Not because she was her sister. She truly was gifted. Effortlessly gracious and always kind, every charity in Atlanta lobbied for her participation. Dad wanted her to join the company's legal team. Any law firm in Atlanta worth a damn had tried to recruit her. She wanted no part of it.

The smartest thing she'd done was run off to New York for a while, avoid the pressure of being constantly sought after. Shelby simply was not going to sit on her hands and let Sara figure Cody out for herself.

She smiled brightly at Sara and Cody. "I was wondering if you'd like to join—"

"No, thank you," Cody said. At the same time, Sara quietly said, "Shut up."

AT LEAST Sara made no more pretense of never having been to the restaurant. As they walked out, several people stopped them to welcome her back to Atlanta, or to ask if she were attending one future charity event or another.

Cody had gotten enough curious looks, no matter how discreet, to make him wonder if she ever dated. Or perhaps the interest resulted because her friends and acquaintances didn't recognize him. He didn't travel in their exclusive circle of Atlanta's royalty.

The evening had gone from bad to worse when he couldn't even pick up the check. Just asking for the thing had earned him raised eyebrows. Sara had to tell him that her family had an account and was automatically billed. Guess handling money seemed too vulgar for the upper echelon. That had really pissed him off.

He was glad to get outside, even though the hot sticky air was stifling and made him feel as if he needed another shower. New York had its share of humidity, but this was ridiculous. He couldn't wait to get back home. Away from this place. Away from…

Shit.

Did he even know her at all?

"Ms. Wellington." Grinning like a smitten twelve-year-old, a valet parker trotted up to her. "I'll get your car right away."

"No, Kyle, I, um, didn't bring it." She moistened her lips and glanced at Cody. She looked so miserable he almost felt sorry for her. Almost. "But if you could call us a cab I'd appreciate it."

"Oh, man, Ms. Wellington, you know how much I like driving that car." He looked meaningfully at Cody. "What a sweet ride, huh?"

She laughed nervously. "I promise to bring it next time. Can you call for the cab now?"

"Sure thing." Cody slipped him a bill, and the young man promptly jogged back to the valet kiosk to do Sara's bidding.

She noisily cleared her throat, and glanced sideways at Cody. Just when he thought she was about to say something, she quickly looked away again. She put a hand to her slender throat, to the spot he'd kissed just hours ago. When he thought she was someone else.

When she'd just been Sara, the woman he'd first met sitting behind the desk in front of Dakota's office. He vividly recalled the first moment he'd seen her. He'd been late for a meeting with one of his partners. On his way to the conference room, he'd stopped by Dakota's office for a file. Sara had just arrived for her first day of work and Dakota was briefing her.

Their eyes had met, hers so innocent and blue

that his heart had actually stuttered. And then Sara smiled, a smile he'd started insanely comparing to the women he dated, to women he encountered on elevators, even to models on billboards.

Shelby's smile was similar, but it didn't light up a room like Sara's. What was it about her? Even now, as frustrated and annoyed as he was, he wanted her.

As they stood near the curb, waiting for the cab, a slight breeze stirred her hair. He wanted to touch the soft silkiness, just like he'd done a hundred times in the past two days. Instead, he waited for her to say something.

But she didn't, which didn't help the situation. It ticked him off even more. Didn't she think she owed him an apology? At least some answers. If Shelby hadn't been there tonight to fill him in, who knows what kind of fool he could've made out of himself. If not tonight, tomorrow, the next day.

In fact, he shouldn't even be here. He should've stayed in Manhattan. He could deny it all he wanted, but he'd come because of Sara. It was about the stupidest thing he'd ever done. Look where it had gotten him.

"Shea, what the hell are you doing here? I must be paying you too damn much."

Great. He recognized Manning's voice coming from behind. Slowly, he turned around. A streetlight illuminated Manning's flushed face, his gaze focused on Sara. Judging by the way he swayed to the left, the guy was also drunk. Again.

"Sara?" The corners of Manning's mouth turned

up in a sloppy grin. "I had no idea you were back. You know I would've called."

"Hello, Harrison." She gave him a tight smile.

Cody raked a hand through his hair. Could the woman have any other surprises? Hadn't he asked her if she knew his client? Good thing Cody had kept his mouth shut about the case.

Manning's eyes stayed on Sara as he approached. "I saw your mother at Arias about three weeks ago. She didn't say a word about you being back. Now, why do you think that is, darlin'?"

As he got closer, Sara took a step back and folded her arms across her chest. "I wonder."

"Come on. You can't still be mad at me. That was almost two years ago."

The bastard started crowding them, and Cody took Sara's arm. "We're leaving now."

Manning blinked and then frowned at Cody, as if he'd forgotten he was standing there. His gaze darted back to Sara before switching menacingly back to Cody. "Y'all aren't here together, are you?"

At the belligerent tone, Cody moved closer to his client so that he could lower his voice. "Didn't we just discuss this kind of counterproductive behavior today?"

"What behavior?"

"You've been drinking."

"What are you, my goddamn babysitter? I don't need this from you."

"Keep your voice down." Cody didn't need to look to know that people were watching. However, this was Harrison's turf, his people. They likely knew this man; whether they forgave his vulgarities was another matter.

Manning got in Cody's face. "I'm so damn sick of your holier-than-thou attitude."

"Harrison." Sara laid a hand on his arm. "Please, don't do this."

At first he wouldn't back down, but then his shoulders seemed to loosen and he took a deep breath, but he didn't take his angry gaze off Cody.

"Where are you headed?" Cody asked him.

Manning's glare became menacing. "You useless prick, you wouldn't even be able to get me out of a speeding ticket."

Cody stared at him for a moment. The guy was hopeless. Manning Senior was too astute a business-man not to realize that his son needed help. Not the kind from an attorney. Anything Cody did for him would only be a Band-Aid.

Ignoring Manning, Cody turned to Sara and slid a protective arm around her shoulders. "Let's go."

Sara huddled close to Cody. He saw the cab pull up a car length away and steered them in that direction.

"You work for me. You don't walk away like that," Manning screamed.

That was it. Tomorrow he'd talk to his partners and withdraw from the case. He'd explain personally to Harrison Manning Senior.

He felt a beefy hand on his shoulder, and stopped. The stupid son of a bitch. Cody took his arm away from Sara and urged her off to the side.

When she realized Manning had followed, she said, "This is ridiculous, Harrison. Everyone is watching."

Cody wouldn't turn around until he got Sara out of the way. He had a damn good feeling he knew what he'd find. "Go get in the cab, all right?"

"No." She looked past him. "Harrison, stop it."

"Please, Sara," Cody said.

"Yeah, get out of here, Sara. Listen to pretty boy."

Cody could feel the guy's foul breath on the back of his neck. Cody sent Sara one final beseeching look. She shook her head and stepped back.

He turned around. The guy wouldn't give an inch. "Harrison, go home. Sober up. We'll talk tomorrow morning."

"Screw you." He drew back a fist.

Cody ducked and Harrison stumbled, nearly landing face-first on the ground. People leaving the restaurant stared in horror.

"You're making a fool out of yourself," Cody warned. "We have a cab. We'll drop you at—"

Harrison lunged at him. Cody had no time to duck. So he did something he'd never done in his life. He punched his client in the face and laid him out cold.

11

FOR TEN MINUTES, Cody and Sara sat in the back of the cab in silence. He didn't even know where they were going. She'd given the driver directions, and Cody hadn't paid attention. He assumed they'd drop her off and then he'd continue to his hotel. When he got there, he'd get on the phone and find the first available flight to New York tomorrow afternoon.

The morning would be busy with explanations and maybe, much to his disdain, a little ass-kissing. Manning Senior. Not the other one. Right now, though, Cody couldn't even begin to process what the fallout was going to be from that absurd fiasco.

Fortunately, Manning hadn't stayed down long, and when he got up he was too disoriented to come back at Cody. The older man in charge of the valet parkers had managed to escort Manning away from the scene. Witnesses seemed to all know Sara and were more concerned about her welfare than stringing Cody up for assaulting one of their own.

He looked over at her. She continued to stare out the window, apparently preferring the darkened landscape to him. Was she embarrassed over the incident?

Too bad. Right now, he didn't much care what she thought.

He was the one who finally broke the silence. "When were you going to tell me?"

She turned to him, but it was too dark to get a good look at her face. "Tell you what?"

"Christ, Sara."

"You just punched out a client. I would've thought that might be foremost in your mind."

"So that was my fault?"

"Of course not." Her voice softened. "Harrison has always been a jerk. I know Mr. and Mrs. Manning. I'm calling them in the morning."

"Stay out of it."

She let her head fall back on the seat. "My family name is Wellington. But for security reasons, I've often used Wells. So has Shelby. I wasn't trying to deceive you."

"No?"

"Deceive is a strong word."

"What do you call lying to me?" he asked, and she turned her head.

The cab pulled to the curb in front of a tall, modern building, probably about forty stories high, and she grabbed her purse.

He didn't recognize the place. "Where are we?"

Sara paid the driver before Cody could stop her. Then she opened the door and stepped from the taxi. He didn't budge and she ducked down to look at him.

"Please, just give me a chance to explain," she said, the pleading in her voice breaching his defenses.

The cab driver twisted around to eye him with impatience. "You staying or going?"

Wordlessly, Cody got out of the taxi and rounded the back of the car to join Sara. "Where are we?"

She sighed. "My place."

"Your summer home?"

Ignoring his sarcasm, she led him to the entrance of the building. Through the glass front, he saw the doorman hurry across the lobby to open the door for them.

"Good evening, Ms. Wells," he said, and then nodded to Cody. "Sir."

"Thank you, Oscar." She walked straight toward the elevators, only she didn't stop there. In the corner was what appeared to be a small private elevator.

"I can buzz you in, Ms. Wells," the doorman said, rushing up behind them.

"No, thank you, Oscar. I've got it." On the wall to the right was a keypad. She punched in a code, and the elevator doors opened.

He followed her inside and she pressed an unidentified button. It didn't have to be marked Penthouse. He was starting to get the picture.

The ride was quick but when the doors opened, he had no doubt they'd ended up on the top floor. There was no corridor, no series of doors leading to different apartments. Only one set of double doors, flanked by two glass panels that prevented viewing beyond the doors. This was indeed the penthouse and it took up the entire floor.

Sara unlocked the door and led him inside. Out

of the corner of his eye, he vaguely saw her toss her purse onto a table or chair, he wasn't sure. His attention was too absorbed by the incredible room. Not so much the contemporary decor, which was pure art in itself, but how the massive windows seemed to bring the city into the apartment. The stretch of city lights seemed to go for miles, yet no other building nearby was tall enough to violate the room's privacy.

"I'm having a brandy. Would you like one?" In the corner, Sara stood at a wet bar the size of some Manhattan apartment bathrooms.

"Sure."

"You have a favorite brand?" She got down two snifters from a glass front cabinet that held an assortment of tumblers and wineglasses.

Behind her, between two beveled mirrors, three shelves were stocked with premium liquor. "Whatever you're having."

"Thank you for coming," she said softly, her gaze on the brandy she poured.

He smiled and checked out the recognizable watercolor on the back wall. He didn't have to get close to know it was the real thing. "You live here alone?"

"Shelby lives here, too."

"And the other apartment? The one with the crazy color scheme and naked pictures?"

She didn't say anything until she brought him his brandy. She handed him the snifter and, looking him straight in the eye, said, "It belongs to my hairdresser. She offered it to me while she was away."

"So you'd have someplace to take me."

She blinked. "Yes."

"I see."

She noisily cleared her throat. "You don't. But I can explain."

He followed her farther into the room where she sat on one end of a curved sofa made from a cream-colored, suede-like fabric. The glass coffee table followed its contours like a piece of a puzzle. He took the other end of the couch.

She kicked off her heels and drew her legs up, tucking them under her and causing her dress to ride up high on her thighs. He doubted it was a ploy, but it momentarily distracted him nonetheless.

"I'm not sure where to begin," she said, looking nervous, giving him a small amount of satisfaction. She took a sip and moistened her lips.

"Tell me one thing first."

She slowly nodded.

"Are you related to Peter Wellington?"

She briefly closed her eyes. "He's my father."

Swirling the amber liquid, Cody stared into the snifter. Thoughts were coming too fast for him to form a coherent response. As if there were one. Peter Wellington was one of the richest men in the country. Came from old money, but had parlayed the modest inheritance into a commanding empire.

The Wellington fortune was so vast that even when Cody had heard Sara addressed by the Wellington name, it never occurred to him that she was from that family. She'd been working as a temp, for God's sake. Remembering the deception, he struggled to rein in his temper. She wanted to explain, and he'd listen.

"I'd like to point out that I did tell you my family had money."

Was she kidding? There was money, and then there was money. He shook his head.

"Everyone thinks it's easy to be rich. They don't understand."

"You thought I wouldn't?"

"I didn't know you. Not until this week."

She had a point. He sipped some brandy.

"When I got out of law school, everyone expected me to join my father's legal team. Frankly, I hadn't thought about doing anything else myself." She gave him a sad smile. "But then I choked."

"Professionally?"

"No, I can do the job. That isn't it. But I realized I hadn't thought out where I wanted to go in life. I had always known I'd go to law school. I love the law. That wasn't a mistake. But practicing corporate law is so impersonal."

Cody agreed. "There's a lot to be said for that."

She slowly smiled. "Just like you couldn't discuss Harrison's case, I didn't feel as if I should offer anything I knew about him that would bias you."

"I was bound ethically. As a friend, you could've given me a heads-up."

Her brows rose quizzically. "Is that what we are?"

He knew she wasn't talking about now, about after what happened tonight. "I don't know."

"We both know what we were doing. As crude as

it sounds, it was only supposed to be about sex. You have a life back in New York that would never have included me."

He stared out of the window at the array of city lights sparkling like stars against the black night. He knew what she was getting at. And she was right. The Sara he thought he knew would have never fit into his life.

"That's why you never asked me out back then."

"You worked for the firm." He met her eyes again, and wished he hadn't when he saw disappointment simmering there. "You're right. I'm an arrogant jerk."

She smiled. "This isn't about you. I'm trying to defend my actions. But now that you mention it…"

He sighed and took another sip of brandy. "You went to Yale, huh?"

"I did. Undergraduate and law."

"I have a friend who went to law school there. Ryan Jordan. Know him?"

"Before my time. But his younger brother, Grant, was a year ahead of me. Now, he is what you call a jerk. Exactly the type of guy who forced me to use the name Wells."

"Yeah, I know him, too. He applied at my firm." Cody knew him, all right. All flash and show, and no substance. He didn't want to work and earn his money. He wanted to marry into it. Sara would have been the prize of a lifetime. Cody didn't even want to know if there was history there.

Sara set her brandy on the side table and looked

down at her hands. "I'm not complaining. I've had many privileges, but they come with a price. When I went to New York, I wanted the anonymity. I wanted to live off of what I made like everyone else. Taking temp jobs was really the only fair thing to do since I knew I couldn't commit to an employer for more than a year.

"The sad thing is, I didn't even make it a year. Eight months. That's all I could take of being stuck in a studio apartment without enough money to buy a decent bottle of wine or go to a play." She briefly looked at him, but only long enough for him to see the humiliation in her eyes. "The few weekends Shelby came to visit were the only times I got to eat in a good restaurant. I hated living like that. I had this big fantasy about learning how the other half lived, and I totally folded. One day I was so broke and miserable that I picked up the phone to hit up my trust fund…" She shook her head. "I gave your sister my resignation the next day. It was over. I'd failed. I came running back to my family's money."

"Hey." He got up and went to sit beside her, taking her hand in his. "What you did took guts."

She laughed without humor. "What? To live like a normal person? Yeah, real gutsy."

"You didn't have to do it. At least you were curious enough to try. That says something."

She sighed, and stayed silent for a few moments. "I'm sorry about Shelby."

"She's your sister. She loves you."

She nodded. "But I want you to know that I didn't have you checked out."

Cody smiled. "I know."

"How?"

"I snuck up on you too quickly."

With a grudging smile, she lightly punched his arm. "What happened? Just twenty-four hours ago, everything was so uncomplicated."

"No, it was complicated. We were better able to ignore it."

Her gaze strayed out the window, and neither of them spoke. He replayed the last few days in his head, and how anxious he'd been to see her each evening. So much so that he'd lost patience with Manning one too many times. Just this morning, Cody had planned on calling the airlines and changing his Friday ticket for an early Monday morning flight that would still get him to work on time.

On the cab ride to pick her up, he'd even gone so far as to think about inviting her to New York for a weekend. Would she believe any of that now? Or would she always suspect his motives?

Finally, Sara asked, "What are you going to do?"

"About Manning?"

"Yes, that, too."

"I've got to call my partners first thing tomorrow morning. Let them know what happened. Then…" He stretched out the tension building along the side of his neck. "I guess I do some groveling." The idea appealed as much as going back to Billy Bob's.

"You'll do no such thing. Don't worry. You won't lose the Manning account."

"This has nothing to do with you."

"I was there tonight, too."

"Yeah, but you didn't punch Manning in the face."

"Only because you beat me to it."

Cody smiled. "That would've been something."

Sara laughed. "I took kickboxing for six months."

Cody automatically touched the corner of his injured eye. "I believe it."

"I still feel horrible about that."

"I'm teasing. But for future reference, is there anything else I should know about?"

"You mean, like my knowing karate, aikido and tae kwon do?"

"No way."

Sara laughed. "Shelby, too, so be careful. My parents insisted."

"Manning is lucky that I'm the one who decked him." Briefly closing his eyes, he stretched out the other side of his neck. "I'll be sure to point that out to his father tomorrow."

"You won't have to talk to Mr. Manning. I promise."

He squeezed her hand. "I appreciate what you want to do, but I prefer you stay out of it."

"Too bad. Harrison has been a pain in mine and Shelby's backside ever since his father started working with my dad. He's lucky we haven't busted him before now."

Cody straightened. "Harrison Manning doesn't— he has his own company. He's affiliated with Wellington Enterprises?"

Regret flickered in her eyes before she looked away. "I shouldn't have said anything."

Panic rose in his chest. He tried to recall if he'd revealed anything compromising about Manning. "Is there a conflict of interest here?"

"No, absolutely not." Looking hesitant, she said, "Mr. Manning had a cash flow problem but didn't want to go public. My dad stepped in and made an offer. It was very private. Operationally, the company didn't change. I shouldn't have said anything. Harrison just made me so mad…"

"I promise it won't go any further."

"Thank you."

"But this is still my problem."

She made a sound of disgust and then put out her hand. "Give me a dollar."

"What?"

She wiggled her fingers. "Just give me a dollar."

Snorting, Cody reached into his pocket and pulled out his money clip. "I have a five."

"I'll take it." She plucked it from his fingers. "Hmm, not bad, a raise on my first day."

He finally got where she was going with this and shook his head.

"Now that I work for you, I think my first order of business will be to give Harrison a call tomorrow morning. Not too early, because I'm sure he'll be hungover. But early enough for him to get on with signing the plea agreement you arranged."

"Any particular reason why he'd listen to you?"

She looked down. "I'd rather not discuss that."

A sick feeling churned in Cody's belly. "Did he…"

"No."

"Sara?"

She looked at him. "He's an alcoholic. He needs help."

The fire burning in Cody's chest threatened to explode. "Did he hurt you?"

"Absolutely not. I would've put him out of commission for the rest of his life."

He believed her. "What happened?"

"It's not relevant."

"You're in my employ," he said dryly. "I'll be the judge of whether it's relevant."

She smiled. "Touché."

He didn't smile back.

For the first time, she looked truly distressed. "Please, I don't want to talk about it. Not right now. This has been a horrible night. Nothing like I'd planned. Can't we try and salvage some of it?"

He knew she was hiding something, and he shouldn't let her get away with it. But she'd scooted closer and the pleading in her eyes melted his resolve. He slid an arm around her shoulders, and she laid her cheek against his chest.

She was right. Tonight had gone straight down the tubes, and all he'd wanted was to have a quiet romantic evening. He'd also wanted to impress her with dinner at La Maisonette. What a joke. He'd been a fool. Nothing he could do or say would ever impress this woman. She already had it all.

She looked up at him. "Are we still on for tomorrow night?"

"What's tomorrow night?"

"*My* surprise." She toyed with his tie until she'd loosened the knot.

He breathed in deeply. The smart thing to do was to stick with the plan. Resolve Manning's case and get on a plane. "What did you have in mind?"

"You have to wear jeans."

He smiled. "And that tells me what?"

She kissed his chin. "It's a surprise."

He couldn't believe what he was about to ask. "What time?"

"I'll pick you up at five-thirty." She almost got his tie off but he stopped her.

"It's late."

She pulled back to look at him, confusion in her eyes. "I doubt Shelby will be home tonight."

"As you well know, I have one hell of a busy day tomorrow."

"I'll kick you out by six-thirty." She bypassed the tie and started unfastening buttons, at the same time, crawling into his lap.

As soon as her sweet curvy bottom hit its mark, he knew it was over, his body and brain at total odds. He shifted his hips, but the friction only made it worse. She teased the seam of his lips until he opened up to her and then sucked her tongue into his mouth.

He found the hem of her dress and slid a hand beneath until he found a garter. Beyond that was smooth silky skin. She squirmed, and he pushed farther until his fingers grazed the elastic of her panties. He made her wait, tracing the elastic with his forefinger, occasionally dipping underneath and brushing the soft curls.

Between her soft gasps and the way she lifted her hips, he didn't know who was being tortured more. He couldn't stand it another second. He had to touch her. Feel her slickness. He put two fingers inside her and she started, her mouth freezing on his. But only for a moment, and then she reached beneath her bottom and unzipped his fly.

He was so hard that with only a minor adjustment his cock sprung to the ready. He started to pull down her panties, but she stopped him. Pushing the strip of material away herself, she then slid down on top of him.

12

SARA STIRRED, hearing a noise like a drumbeat. Soft, yet strong, steady. Startled, she opened her eyes. Her body relaxed when she realized where she was. Laying on Cody's chest. It was his heartbeat against her ear that had woken her.

She smiled and snuggled closer. His eyes closed, his lips slightly parted, still sound asleep, he turned his head so that his beard-roughened chin rested on her forehead. She could easily wake him. One touch. One whisper. But she couldn't be that selfish. No matter that she had every intention of intervening, he had a long day ahead of him.

She had no doubt she could make things right. Mr. Manning could be shortsighted about his only son's faults, but he was a reasonable man. Since Sara had worked on two charity events with his wife, she'd gotten to know the family on a more personal level.

Unfortunately, it had become too personal, as far as Harrison Junior was concerned. He'd gotten the warped notion that she'd been part of the merger package. She'd made the mistake of meeting him for lunch once. After that, for months, he'd called her unrelentingly. She'd never brought it to anyone's attention because her time in New York had ended the calls.

And frankly, she hadn't wanted to deal with the ugly, embarrassing mess. But she wasn't going to keep her mouth shut if it meant damaging Cody's career. She'd call Mr. Manning. They would have a private, civilized conversation, and then Harrison would back off, accept the plea agreement Cody had deemed to be in his best interest. The end.

And then there was Shelby.

Sara wasn't sure what she would say to her sister. The damage was already done. But Shelby had gone too far. Her unwelcome interference had robbed Sara of options, and she was angry about it. Sara should have been the one to tell him when the time was right.

Speaking of which…she slowly lifted herself in order to see the clock behind Cody's broad shoulders. She tried to focus on the digital clock, but the red numbers were still a blur. She blinked a couple of times.

Oh, God. Nine-ten. He wasn't going to be happy. She gave him a shove. "Get up."

"Hmm?" He tightened his arm around her.

"I said get up. Move it, Shea."

He opened one eye.

She gave him another shove. "You have to go."

CODY KISSED SARA, left her at her door, then summoned the elevator while he knotted his tie. She'd offered to drive him to his hotel but he figured that by the time she'd showered and dressed, the cab he'd immediately called would be faster.

Had he totally lost his mind? Thankfully, Manning Senior hadn't called him, not on his cell or at the New York office, but there was no doubt he would. Cody should have been up hours ago making sure he had all his bases covered.

The elevator ride down was quick and when the doors opened, in his haste he nearly ran down Shelby.

She deftly backed up and they managed to avoid a collision. A pair of high heels, probably the ones she wore last night, dangled from her hooked fingers. Her gaze took in his disheveled appearance and she smiled. "My, oh, my. Looks like someone had a long night."

He could say the same except he didn't have time to chat. "Sorry, Shelby, I've got to run."

Her lips curved in a mischievous smile. "Don't tell me you're one of those."

"I really do have to go to work," he said over his shoulder, halfway across the lobby.

"Wait." She sounded serious, so he did, even though he saw his cab pull up in front of the building.

He turned around and she was already walking toward him.

"I'd really like to talk to you. Think you might have time for lunch?"

Taken by surprise, he frowned. "Not today."

"Tomorrow, then?"

He shook his head. For all he knew, he'd be on a plane first thing tomorrow morning. Besides, what more did she have to say to him? Hadn't she done enough damage?

"Or better yet, maybe a drink after work." She

stood close, too close to be casual, and then she adjusted his tie, the back of her hand purposely brushing his jaw. When she lifted her gaze, he knew he wasn't mistaken. Shelby was coming on to him.

Gently but firmly he removed her hand. He looked her in the eye and sternly said, "That's not going to happen."

Shelby smiled, and he realized he'd just passed her test. "Okay, then. Guess I'll see you at the reception."

He liked that she was protective of Sara. "What reception?"

"Tomorrow night at my parents'," she said, and then looked as if she wished she'd kept her mouth shut.

CODY ARRIVED at the Manning offices five minutes before his appointment with Harrison Manning Senior. The man had indeed called him, but had been brief, giving no hint of his intention. Cody had no idea if his firm was about to be fired, or not. As far as Manning's son, he wasn't answering his cell phone. Either he was still sleeping it off, or, more likely, waiting in his old man's office to join in the kill.

According to Dakota, who'd called an hour ago, there'd been no calls from either Manning to the office. One of the partners had left for a long weekend in the Bahamas and the other was in a meeting on Wall Street. Just maybe he could make this whole thing go away before he had to confess his poor judgment. Or perhaps Sara had already fixed things.

He'd firmly demanded she stay out of it, and she'd equally assured him that it was as much her business as his. And he'd be damned if he'd admit it, but he wouldn't argue if she did end up reasoning with Mr. Manning.

"Mr. Shea?" Manning's secretary approached him in the waiting room. She blinked, her look of surprise reminding Cody of his black eye. Terrific. "Mr. Manning is ready to see you."

He got up and followed the short, mature woman to Manning's corner office. The door was already open and as soon as he stepped inside, she closed it behind him. Manning rose from his massive mahogany desk as Cody crossed the room.

They shook hands, and Manning indicated one of the leather chairs across from his desk. "Thanks for coming," he said, looking grim.

From years inside the courtroom, Cody was pretty good at reading people. But he couldn't for the life of him figure out which way Manning was leaning. Since Cody wasn't at liberty to discuss his son's case and Manning knew that, Cody had to guess this was about his firm remaining on retainer. Yet the guy didn't seem angry. More resigned.

"I'm sure you know why I've asked you here." Manning adjusted his silver-rimmed glasses. His graying hairline had receded considerably since the last time Cody saw him in New York about two years ago.

"I can guess."

The older man's mouth curved in a tired smile. He took off his glasses and rubbed his eyes. "I won't ask you anything about my son's case, but I do want to apologize for what happened last night."

"He told you?"

"I haven't spoken to him, but I heard about the incident from an excellent source."

Sara. Had to be. "I assure you, sir, you don't need to apologize for Harrison."

The older man sighed. "You know why I called you here all the way from New York to take his case? Because I'd already used up every other good attorney in Atlanta defending my son over the years."

Cody said nothing. Whether Sara had anything to do with Manning's attitude, Cody knew resignation when he saw it. The man had done what Cody had seen so many rich parents do—coddle their children, never force them to take responsibility—and what they usually ended up with was an adult who'd never grown up, helpless to shake that misguided sense of entitlement.

"He do that to you?" Manning asked with a lift of his chin.

Cody automatically touched the area below his affected eye. "I ran into a hotel valet cart coming out of the elevator."

Manning stared back thoughtfully. "I understand that a plea agreement has been offered," he said and paused, but Cody refused to respond by discussing his client's case. He hoped like hell that information hadn't come from Sara. "Harrison will call you today. He'll apologize, and then he'll accept any recommendation you've given him."

"If you talk to him before I do," Cody said carefully, "you might let him know I'll be leaving Atlanta tomorrow afternoon."

"I'll let him know." Manning stood. "And for the record, there's been no coercion. Your firm has done an excellent job for me."

Cody stood, too, deciding not to comment. He shook Manning's extended hand. "Good to see you again, sir."

"Have a safe trip." His phone rang and he sat back down and answered it.

Cody left the man's office wishing this truly was the end of his dealing with Harrison Manning Junior, but for whatever reason, he doubted it.

At exactly five-thirty, as promised, Sara pulled up in front of the hotel in a red convertible, not any convertible, but a brand-new Bentley Continental GTC, with the top down. Two valet parkers rushed to offer their services. She said something to them and one backed away, while the other opened the passenger door and waited for Cody to climb inside.

"Nice ride," he said dryly as she pulled away from the curb.

"It was a graduation present from my parents," she said matter-of-factly and pulled out from the porte cochere.

She was wearing jeans along with a light blue polo-style shirt. When the sun hit her hair, it was like magic. The blond strands shimmered as the breeze lifted them away from her face. Even in the unforgiving daylight her skin looked flawless.

"By the way," she said, "you look great in jeans."

"I bought them about an hour ago. They're still a little stiff."

"I like my men stiff." She tossed him a teasing look before turning back to concentrate on the road.

A horrifying idea struck him. He stared at her profile, at the perfect, slightly upturned nose, the full lower lip, even the gold hoop earrings she normally wore. She looked like Sara. But of course, so did Shelby.

Sara wouldn't do that to him. Or would she? Turned out, he didn't know much about her at all. He checked the fingernails to be sure. It was Sara. "Where are we going?"

She smiled, but kept her eyes on the traffic, which was pretty brutal at this time of the day. "What part of surprise don't you get?"

"Is Shelby going to be there?"

"God, no." A frown replaced her smile, so quickly, so genuinely, he knew it was Sara. "I had enough of her last night. Anyway, she doesn't like—" She cut herself off.

"What?"

"I almost blew the surprise."

"You're really going to drag this out, huh?" He stretched his arm along the back of the seats so that he could play with a strand of her golden hair.

"Don't be a baby. We're almost there."

He started to pay more attention to his surroundings, but they'd just gotten on a freeway and there wasn't much around of interest. Because she'd told him to wear jeans, he'd guessed that she might have a picnic planned, or maybe they were going to attend a barbecue. But the neighborhoods they were passing didn't look so hot.

What bothered him was that she hadn't brought up Manning. He knew she'd called him. How else had Manning Senior known of the incident last night? Part of Cody was grateful, but the other part of him resented her interference because it made him look weak.

After riding a few minutes in silence, he said, "You called Manning."

"I did. How did your meeting go?"

"How do you think it went?"

Heavy traffic required her concentration but she sent him a quick frown. "You're implying that I threatened him, which I didn't."

"Was I mentioned in the conversation?"

"Briefly. I identified you as my escort, and how embarrassed I was over his son's behavior. I told him that I fight my own battles, and normally I would have taken the matter up with Harrison, but he'd been a problem since before I went to New York and I truly didn't want to have to press charges. I advised Mr. Manning purely as a courtesy."

Cody couldn't help but smile. She'd done good. For him and, in a way, for Manning. Maybe now the guy would be forced to get some help. Daddy wouldn't be there to clean up his messes any more. Cody hadn't heard from the guy today. And since Cody's flight left at noon tomorrow...

It dawned on him that Sara hadn't mentioned

anything about the reception at her parents' house. In fact, she hadn't bothered to ask when he was leaving for New York.

They had disparate lives. They hadn't gotten to know each other until four days ago. There'd be no reason for him to expect her to invite him into her inner circle. It shouldn't bother him in the slightest. But it did.

While she concentrated on driving, he stared out at the scenery for the next few minutes. Finally, he said, "Junior never called today. He was supposed to give the prosecution an answer on the plea agreement."

"The offer expired today?"

"Tomorrow morning. But my plane leaves shortly after noon."

She looked away from the road to stare briefly at him. "You didn't tell me you were leaving tomorrow."

"I honestly didn't think I'd be here this long. The case should have been a simple one."

Her lips turned up in a slow smile.

"What?"

"You didn't have to come to Atlanta at all, did you?" She slid him a glance.

Snorting, he turned to look out the window. She wanted him to admit he'd come to see her. Or was she steering the subject away from commenting on his leaving? He didn't know, and he certainly shouldn't care. His only intention had been to see her a couple of nights while he was here. Of course things had changed. Too fast. He hadn't processed it all.

"Look."

He followed her gaze. Stadium lights were lit in the near distance. "Turner Field," he murmured, and looked at her. "Are we going to a Braves' game?"

"We are." She grinned at him. "Okay with you?"

Was she kidding? Did she understand what this meant to him? "If they're playing the Mets, you know who I'm rooting for."

"I don't think so," she said with a mischievous lilt in her voice.

She exited the freeway but didn't follow the string of cars that headed toward the stadium parking lot. Instead, she swung around the back and followed the fence to where a guard stood at a private gate. She pulled to a stop and he started to approach the car, but then he recognized her. Waving her on, he used a remote to open the gate.

She seemed to know exactly where she was going when she entered yet another enclosed parking lot and found an empty stall between a black limo and a late-model Mercedes sedan. Only about a couple dozen spaces remained in the obviously VIP section.

After consulting her watch, she leaned toward him. "Dinner won't be served for another twenty minutes," she whispered and kissed him.

"Is that right?"

"Yep. How do you think we should spend the extra time?"

He glanced around and they seemed to be alone. But still, sitting in a convertible made him feel more exposed than he'd like. "Maybe by putting the top up."

She bit his lower lip. "Haven't you made out in a car before?"

"Twenty years ago."

Sara laughed. "Oh, you're ancient."

His cock didn't agree. Her scent had been enough to stir considerable interest. He cupped her face in his hands and kissed her in a way that was more private than public. She drew a palm down his chest, to his belt, and just as it got really interesting, they heard a car coming.

Sara straightened quickly. "Okay, bad idea."

"Fine for you," he said when she put her hand on the door handle. "I can't get up right now."

"Oh." She looked down at his lap. "Who wanted to come to this stupid game, anyway?"

He raised his eyebrows at her in reminder, and then smiled. "For what it's worth, this really is a great surprise."

"I hope so." Doubt briefly shadowed her face. "We're having dinner in the owner's box, but after that I usually go and sit in the stands. I like hearing the noise."

They got out of the car and she led the way to an elevator that took them to the top floor overlooking the field. A corridor steered them past several doors, which he assumed led to corporate boxes. He'd been to several at Yankee Stadium sponsored by clients. The food and booze were always of the highest quality, but he agreed with Sara—there was nothing like sitting outside in the stands, listening to the hoots and hollers of the rabid fans.

Not once had he thought about taking a date with him when he'd attended one of those events. The women he knew back in Manhattan would've thought he was insane for asking. Not Sara. She didn't even mind sitting outside on the bleachers. She was an amazing woman. What he knew of her.

The last door at the end of the hall was propped open. Sara led him inside where several people were talking and laughing and sipping cocktails. A waiter passed hors d'oeuvres on a silver tray, and along the wall was a buffet table with chilled bowls of caviar and platters loaded with medallions of lobster and crab claws. Certainly not the typical baseball fare.

The people already inside, one by one, started turning around to greet them. Cody recognized two of the men, although he didn't know them personally; both were on the Fortune 500 list. And no one, not a single person besides Cody and Sara, had worn jeans.

13

"THE SEATS weren't bad." Cody said as soon as they'd made their exit and were heading for the stands.

Sara smiled, glad to hear the teasing in his voice. For not having known anyone at the party, he'd been cordial and engaging, conversing on a variety of subjects.

Yet something was wrong that she couldn't pinpoint. Maybe he was self-conscious about the black eye. Of course no one had mentioned it. They simply wouldn't have been so gauche. "I really hadn't planned on staying up there that long. If you hadn't been so charming, we could've ducked out earlier."

He didn't smile at her teasing. "No problem. I enjoyed it."

"No, you didn't. You're sulking."

"That's ridiculous." He made a sound of exasperation. "However, I do think we could have both dressed more appropriately."

"It's a baseball game. We're sitting in the stands. How much more appropriately could we be dressed?" She stared at his sullen expression in disbelief. Then again, she had to consider this might be about the reception tomorrow night. The one she'd purposely not mentioned, and her *darling* sister had. "Look, it made more sense to wear jeans up there than a suit down in the bleachers."

"You're right."

She stopped to face him when they got out of the elevator. "Is something else bothering you?"

He touched the tip of her nose. "I'm tired. You've kept me up every night this week."

She smiled up at him. "Are you complaining?"

"Hell, no."

"Good."

He opened his mouth to say something but was cut off by a thundering cheer from the crowd. The score had been tied, so it had to mean something big for the Braves.

"Come on." She took his hand and pulled him toward the stands before they missed any more plays.

They found a couple of seats, and then Sara flagged down a vendor and bought the popcorn she'd saved room for. The eighth inning ended with the Braves ahead by a run. Three consecutive strikeouts at the top of the ninth won them the game.

Usually the crowd started to thin toward the end but because of the close score, fans had stayed. Now thousands of people poured into aisles to head out of the stadium and get to their cars so they could wait in traffic.

That was all right with Sara. She was in no hurry to leave. They had to stick around anyway. For the real reason she'd brought Cody to the game.

CODY WOULDN'T admit it to a single soul. Not Sara, not Dakota, absolutely no one. But going to the Braves' locker room to meet the players made him feel like a damn ten-year-old. It was totally absurd that a grown man could be this excited. But there it was. He only hoped it didn't show.

"How do you know *these* guys?"

"I don't know the whole team," she said, laughing, and then more thoughtfully. "Well, I guess I do know most of them. Over the years, Dad has signed endorsement deals with a few."

They waited outside for almost ten minutes because not all the players were showered and dressed yet, and then the security guard waved them inside. Most of the players were still only half-dressed but that didn't seem to bother them or Sara.

"Hey, gorgeous," one of the younger players said, his dark hair wet, a towel around his neck. The rest of them turned around from rummaging through their lockers.

"Hi, guys. Great game."

"Because we knew you were in the stands." A tall lanky man winked at her, and then went back to pulling on a pair of tan slacks. He was one of the pitchers, Cody was pretty sure.

"This is my friend, Cody," she said, linking an arm through his and continuing past a row of lockers and used towels strewn over benches.

They acknowledged him with grunts, smiles, nods. A few guys sized him up as Sara led him past the lockers. The whole thing was surreal. Took him back twenty years when he'd have given anything to be one of them. A Major League locker room, surrounded by players, some of whom would become Hall of Famers.

An unexpected pang of loss gripped him. The excitement from moments ago dissolved into an odd kind of grief. He'd wanted all this once. He'd been good. Good enough that scouts had approached him during his junior year in college, the last year he'd played ball. But he'd already been accepted into law school.

The decision was made, and he'd told himself he'd never look back. He kept telling himself that, all through law school, through the first years of practicing law. Only when he went to a game did he occasionally go back to wondering what if. But in the long run, he was content with his career.

They rounded a corner that led to a small room where two players, looking pretty battered, sat on a bench, their elbows and knees being wrapped by trainers. As Cody and Sara approached, the one with the close-cropped blond hair and husky build looked up and broke into a grin.

"Hey, Sara, you didn't tell me you were coming to the game." He winced when the man wrapping him apparently hit a tender spot on his elbow.

"Hey." The other player with long shaggy brown hair briefly looked up, his eyes bloodshot and his face pale. Then he went back to hanging his head again as the trainer worked on his calf muscles.

"You looked good out there, Joe." Sara let go of Cody's arm, took a seat on the bench opposite the players and then slid over to make room for him. "You, too, Rex."

They both grunted.

"I want you guys to meet my friend, Cody."

Rex kept his head down but looked over at Cody. "I'd shake your hand, buddy, but I'm not sure I can move."

"No problem." Cody watched the pain race across the man's face when the trainer went too deep. "Can't tell you what an honor it is to meet you guys."

"Good to meet you, too." Joe leaned forward to shake Cody's hand, his expression revealing how much effort it took. "Their second baseman clipped me on the shoulder. On purpose, but the damn kid was so fast no one caught it." He grinned weakly at his teammate. "We were never that young and cocky, were we, Rex?"

Rex barely smiled. He barely moved. Not even when the trainer got up and went to work on Rex's neck. He just groaned softly and let his head drop even lower.

"Ouch." Joe flinched and closed his eyes as he got his bicep worked on. "I think the Dodgers are recruiting out of grammar school. That short stop looked like he was twelve."

Rex slowly nodded. "He was fast, too."

These guys probably weren't much older than Cody, but they looked pretty beat-up. Their faces were weathered, their legs and arms scarred from surgeries. Only in their mid to late thirties, and already considered old-timers.

"Yeah, but you guys are smarter," Sara said. "That's why you won."

Joe chuckled. "We won because our basemen and best hitters are twelve, too."

Rex muttered a pithy four-letter word, and then apologized.

"That's okay," Joe said. "You've got good news for us, don't you Sara?"

"I do."

Joe slowly opened his eyes. "Seriously?"

She nodded.

Rex brought his head up and looked at her with a mixture of fear and hope. "Me, too?"

"Yep."

Relief brought life to his face. "Thank you." His gaze went to his trainer and then briefly to Cody. "Thank you," he repeated in a quiet voice.

"I'm gonna be done here in a minute," Joe said, glancing nervously at his trainer. "Then we can talk. Sally and the kids went to get pizza."

Sara smiled. "I think it's better we talk on Monday at the office."

"Oh, right. Yeah, that makes sense." Joe grinned sheepishly. "It's okay if I tell Sally, though, huh?"

"Sure. Rex, I'll see you on Monday, too?"

"I'll be there." He frowned. "Should I bring my agent?"

Sara blinked. "No. That's not necessary." She got to her feet. "We'll talk more on Monday."

They discussed a time to meet, said their goodbyes and then the guys went back to their rubdowns.

By the time Cody and Sara got back to the locker room, only a few players remained. Once they were outside, they saw a couple of them talking to reporters.

"I'm sorry if you felt left out," Sara said on their way to her car. "I wouldn't have dragged you down here if I'd known they were hurting like that. Poor guys. Joe is only thirty-six, and I don't think Rex is much older. Neither of them have a college education. Not pretty, is it?"

Starting to get the picture, he sighed. Maybe it hadn't been his first choice, but he was happy practicing law. Going to work each day wasn't about the money. That was a great bonus he didn't deny enjoying. But the biggest bonus of all was that the legal system truly fascinated him.

She stopped to look at him. "What?"

"I assume that in your own convoluted way you're telling me that they're retiring."

She gave him a wry look before glancing over her shoulder. No one was within hearing distance. "This is the last season for both of them. But they haven't announced it yet. Can you imagine? Not even forty, and your career is over. Not only that, but there's a lifestyle change and—"

"I get the message, Sara."

She warily met his eyes. "I haven't the slightest idea what you're talking about," she said as she continued toward the car.

"It's nice. I'm not complaining." He knew she'd brought him here on purpose. She'd wanted him to see the downside of the game, when a player got too old to play. For some, no more glory, no security, just a lifestyle he didn't want to give up and an uncertain future.

She didn't say anything. Instead she dug out her car keys and used the remote to unlock the doors, a ridiculous move since the top was still down.

He decided to drop it. "You obviously know them pretty well."

"I've been coming to the games for a long time. Since I was a kid, actually. And like I said earlier, over the years some of the players have endorsed products for Wellington Enterprises."

"Is that what the meeting is about on Monday?" The two players were good, but hardly nationally recognized, at least not enough to offer them endorsement contracts.

"I know what you're thinking." She climbed behind the wheel, and he took the passenger seat. "But it's not about an endorsement. We're sponsoring a baseball camp for underprivileged children, and we're hiring Joe and Rex to run it."

"Year-round?"

"Yes." She reversed the car and then they waited for the guard to open the gate.

"Florida in the winter and Atlanta in the summer. We've also started a line of baseball equipment. Joe and Rex will be involved in that, too, with a percentage of the profit used to subsidize the camp."

"You spearheaded this?"

She shrugged a shoulder. "I've done some work on it."

He had a feeling she'd played a major part. "Sounds like a win-win deal."

"Definitely."

Silence lapsed until she got them on the freeway and they were headed back to town. She hadn't said anything about going back to her place or continuing their evening, but of course he'd said nothing, either. For all he knew, she planned on dropping him off at his hotel.

Finally he asked, "How about a coffee or brandy? We can go to the hotel or wherever."

"Okay," she said without enthusiasm. "But I'm afraid it'll have to be an early night. I have a super busy day tomorrow starting at the crack of dawn."

They clearly weren't spending the night together. "Right. The reception."

She didn't look at him but kept her gaze on the road, her smile strained. Shelby must have alerted her that she'd said something. "Mother gets a little high-strung before these events, so I usually help the housekeeper deal with the caterers and florist."

"Hope everything goes well."

"Too bad you have to leave tomorrow."

"Actually, I don't." He could've kicked himself for opening his mouth. Could he have more blatantly fished for an invitation?

The lengthy silence didn't help. "Really?" she finally said, and with a definite lack of zeal, added, "Well, maybe you'd like to come to the reception."

"Thanks, but actually it's best I get back. A week's a long time to be away from the office."

"You won't be missing anything here. It's going to be pretty boring. Mostly politicians and local businessmen on the guest list." She darted him a look. "I wouldn't blame you for wanting to get back home."

He forced a smile. She didn't really want him here. Hadn't he used that line himself at least a dozen times when he didn't want the company of his playmate of the week? Payback was hell.

"But if you'd like to come, Shelby will be there, too."

"That doesn't sound like her kind of thing."

Sara laughed. "Definitely not. But this one's a family mandate."

"Is Carlo going?"

"Oh, no," she said quickly.

Of course not. Like him, Carlo wasn't a member of the inner circle. He wondered if Carlo knew Shelby's real last name. "I'd better keep my flight. I should go into the office on Saturday."

"Yeah, I know it gets crazy."

After a short lull in the conversation, he said, "You realize that tonight could have backfired."

She signaled to get off at the exit and frowned at him. "What?"

"Taking me to the locker room."

She only smiled.

"I'll admit, the initial excitement pushed a few buttons. I started lamenting what could have been."

Her lips parted and she slid him a sideways look

before checking the rearview mirror and then pulling off to the side of the road. They had barely cleared the exit ramp, and he twisted around to make sure they weren't about to get rear-ended.

"We're fine," she said, and threw the car into Park.

"You can't be serious."

"Sara, this isn't the best place to park."

"Tell me that you didn't for one minute think you'd made the wrong decision."

"What's the—?"

"You're a brilliant lawyer. Fair and open-minded and interested in the truth. Anyone who knows you at all knows you're right where you should be." She took a deep breath and stared at him with an earnestness that was humbling.

"I know." He framed her face with his hands and lightly brushed his lips across hers. "I made the right choice."

She readily responded, leaning over the console to kiss him more deeply. He moved his hands to her shoulders and then down her arms. At her wrist, he found her pulse keeping pace with his. Even when a horn honked, they weren't quick to pull apart.

Sara laughed softly, but he could tell she was embarrassed. "The downside to a convertible."

"We could go back to my hotel."

"I don't know."

"Right. Early morning."

"It's not just that." She sat back and put the car into Drive.

"What then?"

"That hotel—I know people."

"Understood." He did, but he wondered why she didn't invite him back to her place.

"I wish you weren't leaving tomorrow." She bit down on her lower lip as she pulled back into traffic. Someone honked because she'd gotten too close, and she waved an apology.

The hell of it was he couldn't tell if her reaction was due to the near miss or because of what she'd blurted out. He figured it was the latter. If he stayed, she'd feel obligated to have him go to the reception.

Well, he was a high-powered, Harvard-educated attorney, goddamn it. He commanded top dollar and had been on Manhattan's most eligible bachelor list four years in a row. If he wasn't good enough to accompany her to a Wellington family function, fine.

He noticed a couple of landmarks that told him they were close to the hotel. As far as he was concerned, they couldn't get there fast enough.

SARA HAD to make a decision. Was she a coward or not? So what that she'd have to explain Cody if he came to the reception. Did her parents think she was a monk? She'd tell them she was seeing someone, whom they didn't know, and they would just have to deal.

Right. There would be a thousand questions. Her time in New York, and her indecision over whether she should join the company's legal team would become suspect. They'd pin Cody under a microscope and then blame him for every wrong turn they thought she'd made. Her parents were good people, and she knew they had her best interest in mind, but they could be so damn paranoid when it came to their daughters. That's why Shelby disappeared abroad so often.

As for Cody, she knew she'd made a mistake by not being honest with him as soon as she'd seen him in Atlanta. Apart from enjoying the whole anonymity thing, she'd never expected him to call again after the first night. But he had called, even when he thought she had nothing, and then he kept calling.

She wasn't foolish enough to think this was a forever kind of relationship, but she did know that she liked him a lot. He might be a snob, but in this short week he'd changed. Would the Cody she knew in New York have stayed one minute in that country and western bar? The thought made her smile.

One more block and they'd be at his hotel. If she didn't make a decision now, it would be too late.

"Would you really change your flight tomorrow?" she asked, turning to him.

He looked wary. "Why?"

"I want you to come to the reception. I want you to meet my parents." She reached for his hand. "I want you."

14

CODY HAD FINALLY gotten the call from Junior at ten-forty-five Friday morning. Definitely a power play on Manning's part, since he didn't know Cody had pushed his flight back to Sunday evening. The good news was that he didn't have to see the guy again. Cody's role with the prosecutor was done. Manning would go in later on his own.

That left Cody with an entire afternoon with nothing to do. Sara was sending a car for him at six-thirty. He understood that she'd be too busy with the caterers to come for him herself. That wasn't a problem, but he sure wished he knew more about the event and the guest list.

His cell phone rang and as soon as he saw that it was Dakota calling, he realized he hadn't called the office to let them know he was staying for the weekend. What was wrong with him?

"I was about to call you," he said by way of greeting, as he stood looking out his hotel room window. Earlier, the sky had been clear and blue, but clouds were beginning to roll in.

"Hey. Are you at the airport?"

"No. I'm staying a couple more days."

After a pause, she said, "Manning won't take the plea?"

"That's done."

"Sara?"

He trusted his sister. She was a lot like him in many ways. She'd been pushed into law school, but ironically she would've made that same choice on her own. Like him, she loved practicing law. Unlike him, she had a satisfying personal life. "Yes."

"Good for you. Stay a month. But whatever you do, don't blow it. She's a nice lady."

"You've heard of Peter Wellington of Wellington Enterprises."

"Cotton manufacturing, sugar refineries, oil, publishing, just about anything you can think of." She chuckled. "Sure, I've heard of him."

"He's Sara's father."

The silence on the other end said it all. When she'd recovered from the startling information, she said, "How do you know this?"

"She told me."

"Wow. I wondered…well, a lot of things make sense now. I always thought she was too smart to be working as a temp, and she always wore killer shoes."

Cody smiled and left the window to stretch out on the bed. "You should see her hundred-fifty-thousand-plus Bentley."

"Boy, do I feel foolish. I kept telling her she should go to law school and if money was a problem, maybe the firm could help her out."

"Yale law. Graduated last year, and she's already passed the bar exam."

Dakota half laughed, half groaned. "What was she doing here?"

"Looking for anonymity. Finding out what it feels like to be a working stiff." At his own words, he smiled and shook his head.

Dakota said something but he didn't comprehend her words. *Working stiff*. To her, that's what he was. A class so far below her own, she hadn't understood the experience.

"Cody?"

"Yeah, um, you know what, I'll have to call you back, Dakota."

"What's wrong?"

"Nothing. The room service I ordered is here."

"Okay, but call me back."

"Right."

"Cody, I mean it."

"I will." He hung up, exhaling sharply, and let the phone drop to the bed. To think he once imagined her to be a social climber, going after a rich husband. What a laugh. Sara Wellington was the real thing. To her, to Shelby, to their parents, he was the social climber.

SARA ARRIVED at her parents' estate shortly after noon and went straight to her old bedroom to leave the new peach-colored cocktail dress she'd wear tonight. Two trucks from her mother's favorite florist were parked on the side drive, which meant her mother was already making Lizzy crazy.

The poor woman had worked for the family for more than twenty years and always managed the staff without a problem. Except when there was a large function like tonight. That's when Sara's normally genteel Southern mother, certain the food would be late and the flowers would wilt too soon, got totally scary. Then Lizzy would threaten to quit. Sara always stepped in and smoothed things over. By the time the party was under way, all was forgotten.

Until the next time. Thank goodness her parents hosted these events so infrequently.

After hanging the dress in the empty closet, Sara stashed her purse on the heirloom walnut dresser next to the glass-enclosed crystal animal collection she'd gotten for her eighth birthday. The room wasn't exactly how she'd left if before going off to prep school at fourteen, but pretty close. After that, she'd only come home for summers and holidays, and then it had been time for college and her visits home lessened. Not because she didn't like coming home. Other interests, like working with the ACLU and a women's crisis center near campus, consumed her time.

She went to the window and surveyed the pool area, where a bar and tables and chairs had been set up. Large potted gardenias had been strategically placed to obscure the pool house. The tennis courts weren't a problem because even though she could see them from the third floor, they'd been built on an area that couldn't be seen from ground level.

Most of the festivities would remain in the house because of the humidity, but for those few brave souls who either liked to venture outside or wanted to smoke, food and drink would be available. Audrey Wellington adamantly did not allow smoking in the house, and that went for the governor. Of course, smoking Cuban cigars in Dad's den was a whole other matter.

Sara sighed. She was not looking forward to tonight. She'd have hardly any time to spend with Cody. Basically, Shelby, who despised attending these affairs, had agreed to be his escort—so he wouldn't have to make his own introductions, and Sara wouldn't have to worry about him wandering around alone.

"Hey."

At the sound of her sister's voice, she spun around. "What are you doing here so early?"

"Thought you could use some help." Dressed in white capris and a pink shell top, Shelby walked into the room, yawning. Her hair was still damp. She'd been asleep when Sara had left their apartment. Shelby had had to do some fast moving to get here so soon.

"Now you're scaring me."

Shelby smiled. "Yeah, me, too." She shrugged and dropped to the edge of Sara's old bed, an antique passed down from their grandmother. "I hate that you're going to be so busy doing Mother's bidding and chatting up everyone that you won't have time for Cody."

"I'm sorry. I really don't mean to burden you with him but I think you'll enjoy—"

"No. Stop it. You're not burdening me." Shelby sighed. "I feel guilty, okay?"

"Why?"

"Mother always depends on you. I understand why. You always come through for them and I'm a screwup and—"

"*You* stop it." Sara sat beside her at the edge of the bed. "You're not a screwup."

"I know. That's what I feel guilty about. It's an act so Mother won't use me to do exactly what you're doing."

Sara laughed. "You think I don't know that? Come on, Shelby, black roses for the Christmas open house?"

"It was a mistake. You don't think I purposely ordered them," Shelby said with mock innocence. Both women laughed. "I knew they'd double-check with Lizzy before they delivered the roses, so it's not like I ruined anything."

"But Mother never trusted you again."

Shelby smiled wryly. "Sorry it came back on you."

"I've never minded. You know that."

"Except today."

Sara stared down at her linked fingers. "I haven't mentioned Cody to Mother and Dad."

"I'm not surprised."

"I mean, I haven't even told them I invited him tonight."

"Lord have mercy, Sara," Shelby said, her eyes wide and sounding remarkably like their grandmother. "He won't get past security."

Sara smiled. "I'm sending a car for him."

"Want me to go get him?"

Sara shook her head. This was so stupid. She was a grown woman. What could her parents say? "I'll do the introductions. At the party."

"Good move. Dad will be too busy to have him checked out."

Sara made a face at her. "I'm sure you can fill him in."

"Look, if I were that serious about someone, tell me you wouldn't have done the same."

"Who said I was serious?"

Shelby's expression softened and she rubbed Sara's arm. "Sweetie, remember who you're talking to."

Sara groaned. "I don't know what I feel. Everything got so messed up."

"How? Tell me."

"I don't know…. I'm not even his type."

Shelby chuckled. "You're gorgeous, intelligent, rich. Sara, you're every man's type."

"Come on, Shelby. You know better."

"I'm teasing, and I wouldn't be if I thought he was someone to be concerned about."

"How can you be so sure he isn't? He avoided me in New York."

"*Avoid* is an interesting choice of words. If he ignored you, that would mean one thing, but avoiding means you scared him."

Sara thought about that for a moment. Her sister had a point. "Yes, but it was clear after he got here that what happened in Atlanta was going to stay in Atlanta."

Shelby's eyebrows drew together in concern. "Did he say that?"

"No, but I knew."

Shelby smiled. "But then things changed."

"Maybe. I don't know. We had fun. Great sex. What can I say? Would I do it over again? Absolutely. But do I know if it's me or the trust fund he's interested in?" Sara shook her head. "I have no idea."

"I think you do." Shelby got up. "If you'd seen his face the way I did at dinner the other night, you'd trust your instincts."

"What do you mean?"

"Honey, he was so upset you'd lied to him, he barely blinked at the fact that you're a Wellington. Come on, before Mother gives Lizzy an ulcer."

CODY SAT BACK in the plush leather seat and sipped from a bottle of Evian as he looked out the limo window. After they'd turned off the main highway, they'd gone nearly half a mile before he figured out they were already on the Wellington estate. A variety of pine and oak trees that flanked the road gave way to well-manicured green rolling lawns.

Another half a mile or so and he saw a small lake, which had to be man-made but looked incredibly natural with the artful placement of boulders and tall ornamental grass. It seemed an odd place for it until he saw that the lake was part of the Wellingtons's private golf course. Nice.

It still took a few more minutes before he saw the black iron gates that presumably separated the main house from the rest of the property. Off to the left was a small brick structure from which a tall husky man wearing gray slacks and a navy blue sports jacket stepped out. Obviously security.

That Cody rode in one of the Wellington limos didn't matter. The driver stopped, lowered the heavily tinted window and through the intercom said to Cody, "Sorry, Mr. Shea, everyone has to stop at the checkpoint. I will have to lower your window, as well."

"No problem."

The driver gave the guard Cody's name, and after the man pleasantly greeted Cody, he gravely looked around the back of the limo, his gaze going to the floorboards and then skimming the stocked bar.

Apparently satisfied there were no stowaways, he said, "Thank you. Enjoy the party, Mr. Shea," and then he stepped back and the gate slid open.

A minute later, Cody could see the house. He mentally laughed at himself. A mansion was a more suitable description. In fact, he'd seen city schools smaller than the massive stone structure that was at least three stories high and branched out into several wings.

Thousands of pink roses curved along the circular aggregate drive that swept around an island garden of miniature trees and flowers. Black-uniformed valet parkers stood at attention. One of the young men was getting into a dark maroon Rolls-Royce parked at the curb and from which an older couple had just stepped out.

Beyond the valet parkers, two white-gloved door-men stood at the entryway between two stone lion's head sculptures. As soon as the couple neared the doors, the attendants, in concert, opened the heavy-looking double doors.

Apart from the occasional pro bono cases that he took, Cody had very wealthy clients. Only the rich could afford his firm. But this kind of money took rich to a whole new level. Before he could open his door, one of the valet parkers had done it for him.

"I'll be parked in back," the driver said. "Either Miss Sara or Miss Shelby will let me know when you wish to return. Have a nice time, sir."

"Thank you," Cody said and got out of the limo.

Behind them, another limo had pulled up and behind it was a Bentley sedan, brand-new, if he wasn't mistaken. Hell, the three vehicles at the curb alone cost more than his Manhattan condo. Of course, this was the Wellington estate. And Sara was a Wellington.

God, he still had trouble believing it.

He walked up the two steps toward the double doors and they were promptly opened. On the other side was a cobblestoned courtyard with a fountain in the middle. Several women in cocktail dresses seemed to be admiring the roses in varying shades of pink and orange that grew profusely around the fountain.

They looked up at him and smiled, curiosity alight in their eyes. He expected he'd be getting a lot of those looks so it didn't bother him. After a polite nod, he continued to the entry doors. Again, there was someone there to show him inside.

He stepped into a two-story foyer that was

larger than his parents' upscale Tarrytown living room. Immediately a waiter approached him with a tray and offered him a flute of champagne. When Cody declined, the waiter indicated a bar farther into the room.

Cody's gaze went to the guests grouped near the bar. Every one of the men wore a tuxedo. Damn it. Sara should have told him.

"Hey, you." Shelby descended the circular stairs, her short red dress showing off her spectacularly long, shapely legs. Of course she looked just like Sara, but he could easily tell them apart. Even before checking out the red fingernails.

"Hello, Shelby."

"How did you know?"

He just smiled. "I hope I'm not going to get kicked out for being underdressed."

She looked him over. "Some of the other men are wearing suits, too." She looped an arm through his. "Let's go get a drink."

He nodded and let her guide him toward the bar. Not that many people were there yet, but he couldn't see Sara. She'd warned him that she'd be busy with the caterers until dinner but he'd hoped to get a glimpse of her. Although the place was so big, with one room appearing to spill out into another, that it would take a search party to find anyone. A series of French doors opened up to a veranda where more guests congregated.

"What would you like?" Shelby asked. "The chocolate cherry martinis are really yummy."

"Uh, no, scotch, please."

"Neat?" the bartender asked.

"On the rocks."

Shelby started to say something but a couple approached and engaged her in conversation. She introduced them, but Cody had already recognized the man. He was Hunter Thornton, chairman and CEO of a Fortune 500 company, who'd been spotlighted in *Forbes* magazine last month.

The couple moved on, but by the time he got his scotch and her martini from the bartender, someone else had snagged her attention. He recognized the woman, a famous European model. For the next twenty minutes, a parade of people stopped them to talk to Shelby. What Cody found so amazing was how many of them couldn't tell her and Sara apart. To him it was so obvious.

"Okay," Shelby said under her breath, her smile still intact. "Let's make a break for the kitchen. Sara will be there and we'll get some peace."

Fine with him. More and more people were arriving, and he was getting pretty tired of making small talk. Mostly, he was anxious to see Sara. He followed Shelby on a circuitous route, which he guessed was the least crowded, and they ended up at the back of the house in a surprisingly small kitchen where three uniformed women worked at the counter.

"Butler's pantry," she said, offhandedly and pushed through a swinging door with a glass window, ostensibly to prevent collisions.

This was definitely *the* kitchen. Two commercial-size stainless steel refrigerators, a series of ovens and a team of a dozen or more culinary staff painstakingly preparing artful salads on individual plates and carving lemon and tomato garnishes.

Away from the fray, Sara stood by the back door, talking with a woman wearing a traditional navy blue suit. But it was Sara who captured his complete attention. Her peach-colored dress was simple, fitted, hit her just above the knees and bared her soft silky shoulders. He'd seen her naked in lamplight, but he'd never noticed how her skin seemed to glow. She couldn't be more stunning.

Shelby nudged him.

"What?" He glanced at her, but his gaze quickly returned to Sara.

"You're drooling."

He sighed, giving her an impatient sidelong look he'd given Dakota a hundred times as a child. Funny how the Wellington twins were identical yet made him feel so differently. Shelby was more like a pesky little sister to him.

"Cody." It was Sara. She waved him toward her. Encircling her wrist was the bracelet he'd given her that last night in New York. "Perfect timing. I have a few minutes." She looked at the other woman. "Don't I, Lizzy?"

Unsmiling, the older woman she called Lizzy regarded him with the open interest of a mother tiger, and then she nodded. "Go. Five minutes."

"I'll see you later." Shelby winked and headed back the way they'd come.

Sara took his hand, and he didn't miss the surprised looks from the kitchen staff. "Let's go outside," she whispered and led him through the back door.

No one was around. In fact, a string of delivery vans blocking the service drive gave them privacy. Smiling broadly, she pulled him along with her until they were nestled between two of the trucks. On one side was the house, on the other dense shrubbery.

She slid her arms around his waist and tilted her head back to look at him. "I'm so glad you're here."

All his worries vanished in the light of her eyes. He touched the tip of her nose. "You didn't tell me it was black tie."

"Oh, it isn't, really. I don't think... Do you care?"

He smiled. Oddly, he didn't. Back in New York his response would have been entirely different. In fact, he would have left immediately. "No."

"Good." She lifted herself on tiptoe. "Because we only have five minutes," she whispered against his lips.

"I have every intention of ruining your lipstick."

She let her kiss tell him what she thought about that.

15

DINNER WAS SERVED in the ballroom, an amazingly large room for a private home, and ended up being a two-hour affair. Cody counted fifteen round tables, each seating eight people and set with fine crystal and blue and white china with the Wellington monogram. Tall tapered candles and exotic fresh flowers made up the centerpieces.

Each setting included four different wineglasses, which meant a different wine with each course. Already he regretted the two scotches he'd had. He was definitely going to have to pace himself.

He still hadn't met Peter and Audrey Wellington. They, of course, sat at the head table, along with a senatorial hopeful and his wife, and several other influential Atlanta couples. He and Shelby sat at a table on the opposite side of the room that Shelby had reserved, ironically, two tables away from Harrison Manning Senior and his wife. Fortunately, their son wasn't present.

During dinner, Sara made two appearances at the table. Once when the tournedos of beef and lamb entrée was served, and then halfway through dessert.

She'd barely been in her seat for five minutes when Lizzy showed up, whispered something in Sara's ear, and both women disappeared.

But it wasn't as if Sara had skipped out on dinner. In between courses, he'd watched her go from table to table, chatting with people, shaking hands, giving hugs, sometimes signaling a waiter to replenish wineglasses. She was the consummate hostess. He could see why her parents depended upon her, while Shelby acted more like a guest. Which seemed to suit her fine. In fact, he'd be surprised if she hadn't orchestrated the roles.

When it was announced that after-dinner cocktails would be served in the parlor while the tables and chairs were cleared away for dancing, Cody couldn't have been more relieved. Shelby had been great company, but he missed Sara. If he had his way, they'd leave now. Go downtown. Her place. Anywhere they could be alone.

"How long do these evenings usually last?" he asked Shelby as they exited the ballroom.

"Too long, as far as I'm concerned. But I think you've already guessed that."

He smiled. He'd gotten to like her in the past couple of hours. Definitely the black sheep, but it didn't seem to bother her in the slightest. "Thank you for babysitting me tonight."

She frowned at him. "You say that like you think you're leaving. If I'm stuck here, so are you. Besides, you haven't met our parents, yet."

"No, I haven't." He was beginning to think he

wouldn't. Shelby avoided them, whether on purpose or by coincidence he wasn't sure, and the few times he'd seen Sara circulating before dinner she hadn't made an attempt at an introduction.

"Come on." Shelby linked an arm through his and drew him toward the fireplace where the Wellingtons stood talking to another couple.

Peter Wellington, a tall, striking man, saw her and waved them into the circle. "Shelby, honey, you remember the Burtons," Mr. Wellington said, and then smiled at Cody.

"Of course." Shelby extended her hand. "How are you? So good to see you both."

Cody wasn't surprised at her grace and elegance. He'd seen her turn it off and on all night. In fact, she'd been an excellent companion, witty, charming, holding her end of the conversation. She just wasn't Sara.

After they exchanged a few pleasantries, Shelby turned to him. "I'd like you to meet Cody Shea. Cody, these are my parents, Peter and Audrey Wellington." She spread a hand to include the other couple. "And the Burtons."

Audrey Wellington blinked. Her eyes were the same vivid blue as her daughters', and her hair identically blond. She was an extremely attractive woman. "Cody," she said, giving him her hand, and looking curiously at him. "Have we met?"

"No, ma'am." He smiled and released her hand. "I believe I'd remember."

Her gaze lingered on his face even as Cody and her husband shook hands. It hit Cody then. His bruised eye had caught her interest. He'd almost forgotten. So far, everyone had been too gracious to bring it up. So was she, but he had to explain. For his own benefit. The last thing he needed was for them to think their daughter had brought home a barroom brawler.

"So, tell us how you met Shelby," Mrs. Wellington said with polite interest, her Southern accent considerably broader than her children's.

Taken by surprise, he hesitated.

"Defending my honor," Shelby said with a perfectly straight face. "That's how he got the black eye."

Mrs. Wellington's pink-tinted mouth formed an O.

Mr. Wellington frowned. "He what?"

Shelby laughed. "I'm kidding."

"Really, Shelby," Mrs. Wellington said in a fierce whisper, giving her daughter a stern look.

Cody sighed. Thanks, Shelby. Great introduction.

"The eye is due to my own foolishness, I'm afraid. I had a tussle with a hotel valet cart."

Mrs. Wellington just smiled, clearly not knowing what to say.

"It was dark," Cody murmured.

Shelby laughed.

"Shea, is it?" Mr. Wellington asked, frowning. "What is it you do, Mr. Shea?"

"I'm an attorney."

"Oh." Looking confused, Mrs. Wellington glanced at her husband. "You work for our company?"

"No, I'm with Webster and Sawyer in New York."

Only one of the most prestigious law firms in Manhattan, nationally recognized, yet she obviously hadn't heard of it.

Though why would she? These people lived on a level he couldn't comprehend. Their feet barely touched ground. He'd bet neither Peter nor Audrey Wellington had even ridden in a commercial airplane in their lives. Or shopped in a grocery store. Mrs. Wellington hadn't merely married money. She'd come from a fortune herself.

Foolishly, he only now truly understood why Sara had been so careful. He also understood how he'd never be acceptable for her. He wasn't one of their kind. The realization was so humbling the feeling was almost palpable.

"What was the name of that firm, again?" Peter Wellington asked conversationally, but Cody wasn't fooled. By tomorrow, the man would know what Cody ate for breakfast each morning.

"Pardon me, Peter, may I have a word?" One of the gentlemen who had been sitting with the Wellingtons at dinner insinuated himself into the group. "I wouldn't interrupt if it weren't important."

Mr. Wellington sent an apologetic look at his wife, his daughter and the Burtons. He graciously included Cody.

"Go ahead. We'll see you later." Shelby took Cody's arm again and steered him away before anyone could say anything. She took him straight to the nearest bar.

They both ordered a liqueur, and while they waited, she said, "My parents are really wonderful people. Their philanthropy is known worldwide." She sighed. "But I'm afraid they don't know many people in the real world." She accepted the drink the bartender handed her and she winked at Cody. "I think it's their generation."

"Hey." Sara walked up just as the bartender gave Cody his drink.

"Hey back." He offered her the Frangelica, but she shook her head.

"Maybe you should take it," Shelby said. "Cody just met Mother and Dad."

Sara's eyebrows went up. "What?" Her gaze darted to Shelby. "Oh, God. What happened?"

"Nothing." Shelby grinned. "It was all very civil."

"You're a pain in the ass, you know that?" Sara said close to her sister's ear.

"Is there something I should know?" Cody asked. "Like perhaps your father has a shotgun?"

Shelby grinned. "Mother keeps it under her side of the bed. Now Dad, on the other hand, has a team of private investigators who'll probably rip you to shreds."

"Shelby!" Sara gave her a warning look.

"Lighten up, Sara. It's the truth, and he might as well know it. Have a drink."

Sara shook her head at the bartender who appeared at the ready. "The music is going to start any minute and the caterers are cleaning up. Then I'll be able to—"

Someone called her name and she turned. A young man, Cody guessed in his mid-twenties, approached them. Sara turned back to Cody and Shelby and excused herself.

This wasn't the first time they'd been interrupted. In fact, it had happened all evening. Every time Sara threw him a crumb, someone commanded her attention. But it no longer bothered him. He finally understood her role here.

"I don't know how she could be so nice to him." Shelby didn't try to hide her disdain as she watched her sister embrace the man. "The guy's a twit. New money, you know?"

Cody just smiled. What in hell was Peter Wellington going to think of her daughter's beau? That he was a Yankee, first off, and right after that he'd discover Cody wasn't on the Fortune 500, not even in the Fortune 1000. The "real world" would consider him very well off. The Wellingtons would find him as insignificant as their pool boy.

"Come on." She reached over the rim of the bar and grabbed an uncorked bottle of Tudor pinot noir. "She's going to be a while."

"I'd rather wait."

"Don't worry. Evan is no competition."

"That's not what I meant," he muttered.

Shelby laughed. "You can learn more about Sara from me than anyone in this room."

Shamefully, he took the bait and followed Shelby. She led him up the semicircular staircase that took them to a balcony overlooking the parlor and the outside courtyard.

"Shoot, I forgot glasses." She shrugged and took

a sip. When she passed him the bottle, he shook his head. She set the bottle down on the floor, and then placed her elbows on the railing. She linked her fingers together where she rested her chin. "See that guy over there. The one wearing a red bow tie?"

Cody followed her gaze. Tall, early thirties, the man looked familiar.

"Logan Masters III, Yale graduate, first in his class and heir to his grandfather's shipping company. We're talking mega bucks here. Now him, I would consider competition."

Cody turned back to her. What the hell was she doing?

"Oh, and William Hartford over there. You might not recognize him. He's Senator Hartford's son. His mother is the one with money, though. Smart guy, good-looking. And surprisingly nice. Frankly, I'm astonished Mother hasn't already ordered the wedding invitations.

"And then of course, there's—"

"Why are you doing this?" Cody didn't understand the sudden transformation. He knew she wasn't drunk. She'd been a great companion. Was this a ploy to send him out of Sara's life?

Shelby pushed away from the railing and straightened. "If you want my sister, you're going to have to fight for her." A slow smile curved her lips. "It's just that simple."

Cody stared out at the guests. "Simple, huh?"

"Look, my sister's crazy about you. But she's scared."

"Why?" he asked, even though he knew the answer. He wasn't good enough. Not for people with this kind of money and power. They didn't marry down. He felt like a fool for having shown up.

"Dad wants Sara to stay with the business and, poor baby, she wants to do what she feels is the right thing by the family."

"What about you? Aren't you pressured?" Had they planned this? Had Sara asked Shelby to do her dirty work? Explain the naked truth so he'd go away quietly?

"They've given up on me. I haven't done a thing they wanted since I learned the word no. Unfortunately, Sara's too nice. She shoulders the burden for both of us." Shelby turned to meet his eyes, and he could tell she was serious. "She deserves more. She deserves to have a happy ending. The only thing you have that these other men don't is that you love her. So if you want that to mean something, you sure better make your move. Otherwise, I'll call for your car."

SARA FINISHED with Lizzy and the caterers, wondering how so much could go wrong after all the planning. Part of it was that she was off her game, trying to keep an eye on Cody.

The other part was that she was a nervous wreck. She wanted to be mad at Shelby for introducing Cody to their parents, but how could she? There had been plenty of opportunities, the caterers be damned, if she'd wanted to take them. But every time she headed that way, her fear got the best of her.

It wasn't that she was ashamed of Cody; she

wasn't. But she wanted her parents to like him more than she'd wanted practically anything.

She knew they'd have objections that had nothing to do with him as a person, which wasn't the least bit fair. They wanted her to be with someone like her father. Someone from old money, preferably someone from the South. They wanted to know the family and, in a perfect world, own something his family wanted.

"Sara, is that you, darlin'?"

Sara's stomach clenched at the slurred words of the one man who was never supposed to have come to this party. She immediately cast her gaze around the room, trying to find Cody and Shelby, but they weren't to be seen. She put on her party face and turned. "Harrison. What a surprise."

He stood by the blue fireplace, his arm on the mantel, a drink in his hand, looking her up and down as if she were a filly at the Kentucky Derby. "Don't you look nice."

She stepped closer to him, making sure there were no other guests within earshot. "Don't you sound drunk."

He laughed. "You're an asset to the family name, Sara Wellington. Truly. So what are you doing, playing footsie with that insufferable lawyer?"

"Oh, Harrison. Some things never change, do they?" She squared her shoulders as she studied the pitiful excuse of a man. "Does your daddy know you're here?"

He rolled his eyes, and she knew he only kept

himself upright by hanging on to the mantel. "Speaking of…your father's never going to approve of him, you know. Not in a million years."

"You don't know my father. In fact, you don't even know your own."

"Don't try and change the subject, Sara. You've dabbled with the other side of the tracks in New York, but it was all right, because your father knew you couldn't stick it out there. And he was proved right, wasn't he? You didn't make it the full year. Not without dipping into the trust."

"You're drunk, Harrison. I'll ask one of the valets to see you home." She turned to leave the room, but he caught her arm just as she was about to walk away. She gasped, never believing a man in his shape could have moved so fast.

"We use his kind to get us out of our little messes," he said, squeezing her arm as she spoke. His vile breath made her wince, but his words were like arrows. "He's not one of us, Sara, and you know it. You think he's exotic and different, which is well and fine for a bit on the side, but don't fool yourself. It'll be just like New York. The novelty will wear off, and all you'll long for is the comfort of home. The comfort of what you've always known.

"But a man like that, a climber like Cody Shea? He's like kudzu, darlin'. He's going to choke the life right out of you, and he's not gonna let go without a fight."

She jerked her arm from his, knowing it was going to bruise. "Your car must still be near the front. You should have no trouble getting home."

Her eyes burned as she walked into the other room, away from the horrible man and his horrible words. Cody was not a trifle. He was not a novelty. She hadn't even realized until this very minute that she didn't just like Cody Shea, she loved him. She didn't give a damn what her parents said about their relationship, either.

In time, they'd get to see the real Cody. The man Sara knew him to be. Her only regret was that she'd been so slow to realize that while she'd been so busy calling Cody a snob, she'd ignored her own prejudices. She should have told him immediately who she was, and why she'd been in New York. He would have understood completely. It was only her fear that had gotten them into trouble, the tiny voice inside her head that had sounded more like Junior than she cared to admit.

"Sara, don't you do it," Harrison called out. "Mark my words, he'll tear you down. In the end, he'll hate you. He'll hate you."

She knew people were staring, and that talk of Manning's display would be on everyone's lips before the night was through. Her training kicked in, and a smile was on her face before she cleared the doorway.

Head held high, she went straight to one of the waiters and asked him to call for the head butler. Then she turned to the first party she saw. Bill Hartford stood with a couple of other Yale graduates, some friends from Andover. At least they weren't strangers.

"Y'all have enough champagne?" she asked as Bill moved aside to let her into the circle.

"Marvelous party, Sara," Jean Longford said. "And don't you look like a picture."

Bill lifted his glass. "I'll toast to that. You get lovelier every time I see you."

"Thank you," she said, wishing she had a drink of her own. "But I've been terrible about calling since I got back from New York. What has everyone been up to?"

Out of the corner of her eye, she caught sight of Joseph. He looked her way and she nodded toward Harrison, who'd parked himself near the bar.

Joseph hardly needed the help. Harrison Junior was as infamous for his drinking as he was for wasting his father's money. It was all she could do not to follow Joseph and Harrison out to make sure he was taken far, far away from the party.

But she was a Southern girl, so she listened to Bill tell her all about his internship. She laughed when she was supposed to and looked impressed when he'd finished. She even touched his arm in the way that Southern girls do.

But Sara yearned to find Cody. To steal away with him and take comfort in his arms. The party could go on without her now that the meals were finished, right?

She laughed again as Bill made another joke. But now that Harrison was gone, she could look around, get her bearings. She turned to her right, careful not to be too obvious. There was her mother, talking to Miss Eve, an old doyen who loved her parties like she loved her gin.

To Sara's left was a group from the stables. The

horsey set always stuck together, no matter what the situation. She should know; she had been one for several years, until she'd been thrown from a horse and her parents had put an end to her Olympic hopes.

Bill brought her back into the conversation with a question about New York. It took her a moment, but she found an amusing story to tell.

What made her look up to the second floor, she couldn't have said. It wasn't his voice, or Shelby's. Maybe a feeling? A sense that she was being watched?

The laughter at her story was still in the air as she stepped to her left and looked back, then up. The moment she saw Cody, Bill put his arm around her shoulder.

That wasn't the worst of it, though. Because she'd stood up there, many times before, at the very spot where Cody was staring down at her. And she'd heard every word spoken, all the way to where she was right now.

She knew in an instant that Cody had caught what Harrison Manning Junior had said. It didn't surprise her when Cody walked down the staircase and headed toward the front door.

She should go after him. Explain. Tell him that she didn't believe a word Junior had said. Dammit, she should tell him that she loved him. That they belonged together.

Only she didn't. Because what if Junior was right? Not about Cody, but about her?

16

A SOON AS CODY got outside he remembered he had no car and no means of quickly finding one. He'd depended on Sara to get here, and then on Shelby to get him through the evening. He was a joke, and he couldn't even think straight.

"Sir, would you like your car brought around?" A valet parker trotted up to him. Behind the man, near the magnolia tree, Cody recognized the driver leaning against the limo that had brought him here.

"Yes, thank you," he said, loath to depend on the Wellingtons for a single thing. But getting the hell out of here was priority number one.

He waited impatiently as the valet gave the signal and the driver got behind the wheel. It took only a minute to navigate the circular drive and stop in front of Cody. Long enough for Cody to wonder how long the driver had been waiting there. Sara hadn't had time to call for him.

Cody climbed into the back, his head pounding with humiliation. Had she hoped to be rid of him before now? Was that why the car had been ready?

Screw her. Screw the Wellingtons. Harrison Man-

ning could rot in jail for all he cared. The stupid
bastard was nothing but a worthless drunk. Sara
should have screamed at him for the things he'd said.
But she hadn't. She'd stood there and taken it all. In
front of everyone. Most likely because Manning had
told her the truth.

He loosened his tie, and then jerked it off from
around his neck. So roughly that he lost a button.
Anger threatened to cut off his air passage. Was he
so arrogant that he hadn't seen this coming? The
rich were different. He knew that. Goddamn it, he
knew that. What had he really expected?

It was too dark to see anything; still, he stared out
the window. Sara hadn't wanted him to come to the
reception. She barely wanted him to know who she
was. It was only her polite upbringing that had forced
the invitation, and he was too much of a yokel to have
seen it.

His jaw was clenched so tight he had to force
himself to relax. He had to think about what to do
next. Besides get the hell out of Atlanta. The Manning account wouldn't be affected by Harrison
Junior's diatribe. Except for the embarrassment
factor. Manning could pull his account just so he
wouldn't have to face Cody again.

The truth was, he couldn't care less about the potential business fallout. He hadn't even cared about
schmoozing with the powerhouses at the game last
night. Two weeks ago, he would've milked every
contact he'd made. Charmed his way into a retain-
ing fee or two. But when he was with Sara, business

seemed to fade into the background. Sara was all that mattered.

Turns out, he was only her temporary distraction. A burger and fries in a life filled with caviar. Come on, going to the country and western restaurant, eating the onion rings. It had all been a lark for her, a game.

How she must have laughed when she'd opened that Tiffany box. She could buy him, his company, and everyone he knew without breaking a sweat. She probably wore pink diamonds when she jogged.

He laid his head back, tightly shutting his eyes. They burned like hell. In the last five days he'd barely had any sleep, gotten a black eye and almost lost an important client. When was the last time a woman had captured his attention to the point he'd been blinded with lust?

Never. Only because there hadn't been anyone like Sara before.

Damn her.

Why had she even bothered wearing the bracelet? To think he'd wanted to impress her with the gift. No wonder she'd been so subdued. It had all been part of her slumming adventure. How many possible ways could he prove what a damn fool he was?

He opened his eyes and stared out into the blackness. No moonlight. No stars. The sky was empty. Just like he felt. If only he hadn't come to Atlanta. If only he hadn't been inside Sara and watched her smile. Because now, going back to his pathetic life, to empty relationships with vapid women who were all interchangeable, was going to be the hardest thing he'd ever done in his life.

How would he ever do that? Just walk away from Sara, and know he'd never see her again. How? How could he possibly do that?

Shelby's words came back to him. She'd told him he had to fight for Sara if he loved her. Well, did he? Was this thing he felt worth fighting for?

The answer was a fast, unequivocal yes. And with that yes, he straightened his shoulders as his heart started to race. Who knew Sara better than her twin? She'd said Sara was scared. She'd also said Sara loved him.

If he let his pride get in the way and walked now, how could he look himself in the mirror? That alone would make him unworthy of Sara.

For the first time in his life, he didn't give a damn about decorum or appearances. Everyone at the party had already heard what Manning had to say. Now they were going to hear from Cody.

He leaned forward and raked a hand through his messy hair. "Driver, we need to turn around."

SARA SMILED and laughed with the guests until she thought her face would crack. Shatter into a million pieces, just like her heart had done the minute Cody had walked out the door. How he must hate her for being so weak.

Of course no one had said a thing about the incident. Not to her face, anyway. However, by tomorrow at breakfast she'd be the hot topic of conversation. Even among the household staff. Mother hadn't said a word yet. In fact, she'd stayed in one of the other rooms chatting with her tennis partner. No doubt she'd have plenty to say later about how common and embarrassing the display had been. She wouldn't fault Harrison. She'd blame Cody.

The thought angered Sara to the point that she had to excuse herself and head for the kitchen. Most of the caterers had left, along with most of their mess. Maybe she could find a quiet spot, if only for a few minutes.

Shelby entered the kitchen right behind her. Two of the staff were still cleaning up, even as another pair were refreshing the drink trays. Shelby grabbed Sara's arm and walked her into the butler's pantry.

"Don't those people have homes?" Sara said a tad too loudly. "It's late. The party should be over."

Shelby laughed. "What happened to your Southern hospitality? Besides, it's the shank of the evening. These people won't go home until the last drop of champagne has been poured."

"How can you think this is funny?" Sara's voice caught on a sob.

"Sweetie, I'm on your side."

Sara shook her head, trying her best not to cry. All she needed was to feed the rumor mill by going back out there with smudged eye makeup. "How could you let Cody hear that vile Harrison?"

"How could I have stopped it?"

"I don't know. You could have let me know you two were up there."

"Right."

Sara sniffed. "It's my fault. I totally blew it."

"No, you didn't," Shelby said firmly, and then narrowed her gaze. "Unless what Harrison said is true."

Sara remained silent. She owed it to herself to give the possibility some thought. But there was simply no other answer in her. "No, it's not true. I might be spoiled and too used to the privileged life we have, but I know that Cody is worth more to me than any of it. He's not who people might think I should date, and that's okay with me. *I* want him."

"That's all that matters," Shelby said. She touched her sister on the cheek, brushing away one of her tears. "It may seem awful right now, but you know what? I'm so jealous I could scream."

"What?"

"Sara, he's a really good guy. Do you think for one minute if he were after you for your money he'd have walked out that door? He left because he's afraid he's not good enough for you. Your job now is to convince him he is."

"He's probably halfway to New York already."

"Somehow I doubt it." Shelby smiled. "Now, get your privileged ass in gear and go find the man."

"What about the party?"

"Don't worry about it. I'll make sure nothing goes wrong."

Shelby's hands went to Sara's shoulders, and she shoved Sara toward the door. "Go. Trust me. I know what to do."

"You're sure?"

"Sara Wellington, if you don't leave right this instant—"

"All right. I'm going. I'm scared spitless, but I'm going."

Shelby's laughter followed her through the kitchen, but when she got to the main hall, she was alone with her fear. It might be too late, and then what? Live the rest of her life knowing she'd found the right man, but had been too foolish to see the truth in time?

She touched the bracelet on her wrist as she hurried past guests and parents and ex-boyfriends. All the people who had been so important in her life. None of whom could possibly console her if she lost Cody Shea.

"Sara—"

"I can't stop now, Mother. I have something to do."

"Sara!"

"I'll explain later," she said, twirling in an inelegant circle before she faced the front entrance again. "Just wish me luck."

She didn't wait to hear her mother's exasperation. It didn't matter. Neither would their initial reaction, if she managed to bring Cody home. In time, they would see what she saw. They'd grow to love him, and if they didn't? No, they would.

The worst of it would be from her father. He expected her to work for the company, to live here in Atlanta. But if she and Cody… If they…

Oh, why had she worn heels? It felt as if she had

to trek through three states to get to the front door. She stopped, took off her shoes and, holding them in her left hand, she started again.

But everyone at the party seemed to want to stop her. She made every polite excuse she could until she reached the foyer. With the door in sight, she had no more graces left. Had he checked out of his hotel? Should she go to the airport? Of course not. He hadn't been gone long enough. Damn, she had no purse. No phone. No license. She'd have to borrow a driver, and that would make things more difficult. Oh, she couldn't cry now. Not when she was so close.

She slowed by Mrs. Kellog, who was a little too old and deaf to hear Sara's excuse as she passed. It was okay, though, because as Sara turned toward the front door, everything changed. She struggled for a gulp of air.

Cody had come back.

He had no tie, his shirt was askew, his hair was a mess, and he was the best thing she'd ever laid eyes on. He got closer, but she wasn't sure if it was her moving or him. Maybe both. All that mattered was that he'd come back. After her being such a dope, he'd come back.

"I have something to say." Cody stood a few feet away, far enough that he couldn't touch her but close enough for her to see the intensity and purpose in his eyes.

She blinked back her tears. She had so much to say herself, but it wasn't time yet. Now, she needed to listen.

"You asked me once why I came to Atlanta. Why I personally came down to babysit that idiot. I came because I had no choice. You did something to me, Sara Wells, I mean, Wellington. You made all the other women in the world pale in comparison. You made the rest of my life seem uninteresting. You changed the way I wake up in the morning. How I think about mornings at all. I'm in love with you. There's not a thing I can do about it, except tell you, finally, that I don't want to spend another day without you."

He took a step closer, but he wasn't finished, and he didn't touch her. He did, however, look so deeply into her eyes that he had to see the truth there, didn't he?

"You can have any man in the world, and there's no reason on earth you'd choose me. But if you do, I know I can make you happy."

"Are you done?"

He slowly nodded, his gaze never leaving hers.

"I love you right back," she promised. But she wasn't satisfied at that. Not when in three steps she could be in his arms.

Make that two.

His arms went around her waist and he lifted her into his kiss. She knew she was weeping all over the place, but she didn't give a tinker's damn.

"I love you," she whispered against his lips.

"We fit," he replied with a relieved smile.

"Yes, we do." She kissed him so hard he stumbled backwards.

When he finally put her down and she could breathe again, she looked past Cody and laughed.

"What?" he asked.

"Don't ever discount Southern manners," she said. Everyone at the party had cleared the room. No one had made a peep, they'd all gone and given Sara and Cody their moment.

Except then she saw her mother, standing in the doorway to the ballroom, her lips parted in that appalled look of hers.

Sara gave her a bright smile, her heart lighter than she could remember it ever being. Mother would get over it. She'd just have to.

"Did I just totally embarrass you?" he asked softly.

"Totally. You must take me away from here. Now." She gave him a wicked smile, grabbed the front of his shirt and, with their gazes locked, led him into the courtyard.

Bless Shelby, Sara's car waited at the curb. She pulled him closer. "Your place or mine?"

Epilogue

Two years later

"WHERE WOULD YOU LIKE to go for dinner tonight? Maybe that new sushi place that opened off Lexington?" Cody slid his arms around Sara's waist and brought her back against his chest while he watched her face in the mirror.

She took off first one gold hoop earring and then the other and set them on the vanity table. She wouldn't meet his eyes. Something was wrong. "I was thinking we'd eat in tonight."

"Okay," he said slowly. "How's the case? Did Judge Saunders turn down your motion to suppress the search?"

"No." Smiling, a little too brightly, she turned to face him. "I don't think we'll have to go to trial."

"Something's wrong, Sara."

Her smile faltered, and she glanced away.

Cody's chest tightened. He'd dreaded this day. For nearly two years they'd lived in his Manhattan condo. He'd stayed with his firm, and Sara had used part of her trust fund to open up a small office where she took only pro bono cases.

So far, they'd done quite well on his salary. They even managed to visit her family in Atlanta at least every other month. But deep inside he'd wondered if the day would come when she'd miss home. Become bored with their lives.

"Sara, please. What's wrong, baby?"

She sighed. "It's Mother."

"Yes?" He thought they'd made peace. He'd even thought she'd started to like him.

Sara turned away and cleared her throat. "Look, I know we've never really discussed this but…" She spun around to face him again. "You know, I think sushi sounds good, after all."

"Sara."

Her lips quivered. She pressed them tightly together, keeping her gaze on him. "I'm just going to say it." She briefly closed her eyes and then blurted, "Mother's been making noise about a wedding."

Stunned, Cody stared at her.

"I mean, everything is fine as it is, so don't feel like you have to—"

Smiling, Cody picked her up and swung her around. He loved this woman more than life itself. Didn't she know he'd do anything for her? If she wanted him to quit his job and move to Alaska in the middle of winter, he'd do it. In a New York minute. "If that's a marriage proposal, I accept."

She smacked his shoulder, tears already shining in her eyes. "You know Mother's going to make it a big honkin' affair."

"That's okay. But only if it's what you want," he said, and hugged her tighter.

"I'd really like a small wedding like Dakota and Tony had last summer."

"That was small? Tony has more relatives than the Bronx and Brooklyn have residents."

"To Mother, that would've been small."

"Then we'll put our foot down."

She grinned. "You'll talk to her?"

"Honey, I'd challenge Shelby to a duel to make you happy, and you know how scared I am of her."

She laughed. "You should be. She could take you. Lucky for you she just left for Europe again." Sara fixed his tie, and then looked up with love shining in her beautiful blue eyes. "Have I told you lately how much I love you?"

He picked her up again and headed toward their king-size bed. If he lived to be a hundred, he could never hear it enough. "I love you, Sara Wellington. For the rest of my life."

* * * * *

Silhouette® Romantic Suspense
keeps getting hotter!
Turn the page for a sneak preview
of Wendy Rosnau's latest **SPY GAMES** *title*
SLEEPING WITH DANGER

Available November 2007

Silhouette® Romantic Suspense—
Sparked by Danger, Fueled by Passion!

Melita had been expecting a chaste quick kiss of the generic variety. But this kiss with Sully was the kind that sparked a dying flame to life. The kind of kiss you can't plan for. The kind of kiss memories are built on.

The memory of her murdered lover, Nemo, came to her then and she made a starved little noise in the back of her throat. She raised her arms and threaded her fingers through Sully's hair, pulled him closer. Felt his body settle, then melt into her.

In that instant her hunger for him grew, and his for her. She pressed herself to him with more urgency, and he responded in kind.

Melita came out of her kiss-induced memory of Nemo with a start. "Wait a minute." She pushed Sully away from her. "You bastard!"

She spit two nasty words at him in Greek, then wiped his kiss from her lips.

"I thought you deserved some solid proof that I'm still in one piece." He started for the door. "The clock's ticking, honey. Come on, let's get out of here."

"That's it? You sucker me into kissing you, and that's all you have to say?"

"I'm sorry. How's that?"

He didn't sound sorry in the least. "You're—"

"Getting out of this godforsaken prison cell. Stop whining and let's go."

"Not if I was being shot at sunrise. Go. You deserve whatever you get if you walk out that door."

He turned back. "Freedom is what I'm going to get."

"A second of freedom before the guards in the hall shoot you." She jammed her hands on her hips. "And to think I was worried about you."

"If you're staying behind, it's no skin off my ass."

"Wait! What about our deal?"

"You just said you're not coming. Make up your mind."

"Have you forgotten we need a boat?"

"How could I? You keep harping on it."

"I'm not going without a boat. And those guards out there aren't going to just let you walk out of here. You need me and we need a plan."

"I already have a plan. I'm getting out of here. That's the plan."

"I should have realized that you never intended to take me with you from the very beginning. You're a liar and a coward."

Of everything she had read, there was nothing in Sully Paxton's file that hinted he was a coward, but it was the one word that seemed to register in that one-track mind of his. The look he nailed her with a second later was pure venom.

He came at her so quickly she didn't have time

to get out of his way. "You know I'm not a coward."

"Prove it. Give me until dawn. I need one more night to put everything in place before we leave the island."

"You're asking me to stay in this cell one more night...and trust you?"

"Yes."

He snorted. "Yesterday you knew they were planning to harm me, but instead of doing something about it you went to bed and never gave me a second thought. Suppose tonight you do the same. By tomorrow I might damn well be in my grave."

"Okay, I screwed up. I won't do it again." Melita sucked in a ragged breath. "I can't leave this minute. Dawn, Sully. Wait until dawn." When he looked as if he was about to say no, she pleaded, "Please wait for me."

"You're asking a lot. The door's open now. I would be a fool to hang around here and trust that you'll be back."

"What you can trust is that I want off this island as badly as you do, and you're my only hope."

"I must be crazy."

"Is that a yes?"

"Dammit!" He turned his back on her. Swore twice more.

"You won't be sorry."

He turned around. "I already am. How about we seal this new deal?"

He was staring at her lips. Suddenly Melita knew what he expected. "We already sealed it."

"One more. You enjoyed it. Admit it."

"I enjoyed it because I was kissing someone else."

He laughed. "That's a good one."

"It's true. It might have been your lips, but it wasn't you I was kissing."

"If that's your excuse for wanting to kiss me, then—"

"I was kissing Nemo."

"What's a nemo?"

Melita gave Sully a look that clearly told him that he was trespassing on sacred ground. She was about to enforce it with a warning when a voice in the hall jerked them both to attention.

She bolted away from the wall. "Get back in bed. Hurry. I'll be here before dawn."

She didn't reach the door before he snagged her arm, pulled her up against him and planted a kiss on her lips that took her completely by surprise.

When he released her, he said, "If you're confused about who just kissed you, the name's Sully. I'll be here waiting at dawn. Don't be late."

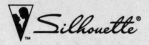

Silhouette®

Romantic
SUSPENSE

Sparked by Danger,
Fueled by Passion.

Onyxx agent Sully Paxton's only chance of
survival lies in the hands of his enemy's daughter
Melita Krizova. He doesn't know he's a pawn in the
beautiful island girl's own plan for escape. Can
they survive their ruses and their fiery attraction?

Look for the next installment in the
Spy Games miniseries,

Sleeping with
Danger
by Wendy Rosnau

Available November 2007 wherever you buy books.

ATHENA FORCE

Heart-pounding romance and thrilling adventure.

History repeats itself...unless she can stop it.

Investigative reporter Winter Archer is thrown into writing
a biography of Athena Academy's founder. But someone
out there will stop at nothing—not even murder—to
ensure that long-buried secrets remain hidden.

ATHENA FORCE

Will the women of Athena unravel Arachne's powerful
web of blackmail and death...or succumb to their
enemies' deadly secrets?

Look for

VENDETTA
by *Meredith Fletcher*

*Available November
wherever you buy books.*

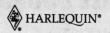

REQUEST YOUR FREE BOOKS!

2 FREE NOVELS
PLUS 2
FREE GIFTS!

HARLEQUIN®

Blaze®

Red-hot reads!

YES! Please send me 2 FREE Harlequin® Blaze® novels and my 2 FREE gifts.
After receiving them, if I don't wish to receive any more books, I can return the
shipping statement marked "cancel." If I don't cancel, I will receive 6 brand-new
novels every month and be billed just $3.99 per book in the U.S., or $4.47 per book
in Canada, plus 25¢ shipping and handling per book and applicable taxes, if any*.
That's a savings of at least 15% off the cover price! I understand that accepting the
2 free books and gifts places me under no obligation to buy anything. I can always
return a shipment and cancel at any time. Even if I never buy another book from
Harlequin, the two free books and gifts are mine to keep forever.

151 HDN EF3W   351 HDN EF3X

Name	(PLEASE PRINT)	
Address		Apt.
City	State/Prov.	Zip/Postal Code

Signature (if under 18, a parent or guardian must sign)

Mail to the **Harlequin Reader Service®**:
IN U.S.A.: P.O. Box 1867, Buffalo, NY 14240-1867
IN CANADA: P.O. Box 609, Fort Erie, Ontario L2A 5X3

Not valid to current Harlequin Blaze subscribers.

Want to try two free books from another line?
Call 1-800-873-8635 or visit www.morefreebooks.com.

* Terms and prices subject to change without notice. NY residents add applicable sales
tax. Canadian residents will be charged applicable provincial taxes and GST. This offer is
limited to one order per household. All orders subject to approval. Credit or debit balances
in a customer's account(s) may be offset by any other outstanding balance owed by or to
the customer. Please allow 4 to 6 weeks for delivery.

Your Privacy: Harlequin is committed to protecting your privacy. Our Privacy
Policy is available online at www.eHarlequin.com or upon request from the Reader
Service. From time to time we make our lists of customers available to reputable
firms who may have a product or service of interest to you. If you would
prefer we not share your name and address, please check here. ☐

HB07

HARLEQUIN *Romance*

New York Times bestselling author

DIANA PALMER

Handsome, eligible ranch owner Stuart York knew
Ivy Conley was too young for him, so he closed his heart
to her and sent her away—despite the fireworks between
them. Now, years later, Ivy is determined not to be
treated like a little girl anymore…but for some reason,
Stuart is always fighting her battles for her. And safe in
Stuart's arms makes Ivy feel like a woman…his woman.

Winter Roses

Available November.

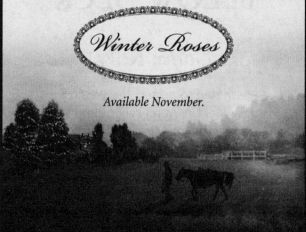

Mediterranean NIGHTS™

*Not everything is above board
on Alexandra's Dream!*

*Enjoy plenty of secrets, drama and sensuality
in the latest from Mediterranean Nights.*

Coming in November 2007...

BELOW DECK

by

Dorien Kelly

Determined to protect her young son,
widow Mei Lin Wang keeps him hidden
aboard *Alexandra's Dream* under cover of
her job. But life gets extremely complicated
when the ship's security officer, Gideon Dayan,
is piqued by the mystery surrounding this
beautiful, haunted woman....

Silhouette

SPECIAL EDITION™

**brings you a heartwarming
new McKettrick's story from**

NEW YORK TIMES BESTSELLING AUTHOR

LINDA LAEL MILLER

THE McKETTRICK
Way

Meg McKettrick is surprised to be reunited
with her high school flame, Brad O'Ballivan,
who has returned home to his family's
neighboring ranch. After seeing Meg again,
Brad realizes he still loves her. But the pride
of both manage to interfere with love...until
an unexpected matchmaker gets involved.

—— McKettrick Women ——

Available December wherever you buy books.

HARLEQUIN®

Blaze™

COMING NEXT MONTH

#357 SEX BOMB Jamie Sobrato
Elle Jameson can wield a .38 as fiercely as a makeup brush. But there's not a big demand for her eclectic skill set. Then Christian Navarro appears to recruit her to a secret spy agency. A chance to use her talents *and* a superhot guy to train her? She is so there!

#358 DEAD SEXY Kimberly Raye
Love at First Bite, Bk. 1
Hairdresser Nikki Braxton has had it with dating losers. So when she falls desperately in lust with sexy cowboy Jake McMann, she's thrilled. Jake is the real deal, a man's man. Too bad he's also a vampire....

#359 DANGEROUS... Tori Carrington
Extreme
When undercover agent Lucas Paretti agreed to infiltrate the mafia, he never dreamed he'd have another chance with his first love, Gia Trainello. Or that his still unbelievably sexy Gia would be the new Lady Boss of the family he's vowed to bring down...

#360 WILD CHILD Cindi Myers
Sex on the Beach, Bk. 3
Sara Montgomery needs this vacation in the biggest way. But getting unplugged from the cell phone and laptop is proving tricky. Luckily for her, hottie surfer guy Drew Jamison arrives as the perfect distraction. Who can think about work with this kind of temptation?

#361 FEELING THE HEAT Rhonda Nelson
Big, Bad Bounty Hunters, Bk. 1
Bounty hunter Linc Stone always gets his man. But when irresistibly sexy Georgia Hart joins him, insisting on helping him track down her louse of an ex-boyfriend, Linc can't help thinking he'd like to get his woman—*this* woman—too. Into bed, that is...

#362 TALL, DARK AND FILTHY RICH Jill Monroe
Million Dollar Secrets, Bk. 5
"There's always dirt." That's female P.I. Jessie Huell's mantra. But when she uncovers a serious scandal involving Cole Crawford—her long-term crush—will she be so quick to reveal it? Especially when it might ruin her shot at finally bedding the gorgeous TV producer?

www.eHarlequin.com

HBCNM1007